MGH in Bloom

DORIS M. DORWART

authorHOUSE®

AuthorHouse™
1663 Liberty Drive
Bloomington, IN 47403
www.authorhouse.com
Phone: 1 (800) 839-8640

Published by AuthorHouse 06/14/2017

ISBN: 978-1-5246-9601-6 (sc)
ISBN: 978-1-5246-9599-6 (hc)
ISBN: 978-1-5246-9600-9 (e)

Library of Congress Control Number: 2017909103

Print information available on the last page.

This book is printed on acid-free paper.

ACKNOWLEDGEMENTS

E very time I sit down to write and think that I'm in command of what goes into my stories, my characters seem to take control. They begin to act and speak in surprising ways. So, I have learned to let them guide my fingers on the keyboard.

In *MGH in Bloom*, one character becomes a hero in spite of himself. I always had a soft spot in my heart for this character and now I understand that I had a glimpse of his goodness all along. I hope you, too, will feel this way after you have read the book.

My thanks to Jane Lloyd, my editor, for her fabulous ability to help me strengthen my story lines and make my characters come alive on the printed page.

To Gina Schaeffer, the mother of Joshua and Ellie, two of my great-grandchildren, my compliments on the art work she created for the cover of this book. You came through again!

Special thanks to my sister Geraldine Wagner for her patience in taking my phone calls when I am frustrated, and I have lost faith in myself. Special note to you, Geri— because of you, I do not have to pack my bag and go over the hill!

CHAPTER 1

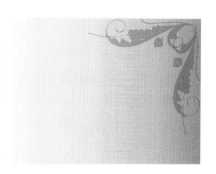

Hortense King Ferndale was in her office at Morning Glory Hill, an elegant, independent living residency, waiting for two women, who had made an appointment to view the facility. She was proud of the new name plate appropriately displayed on an ornate walnut desk in her well-appointed office. While she had been serving as the director of this relatively new facility for over a year and a half, she had only recently married and was still trying to get used to being called Mrs. Ferndale. She had been single so long that she had almost given up on marriage as an option for her. Then along came Claude and her world had not been the same since then.

A long time ago, Hortense realized she had to make the best of what she had. Her complexion was flawless—no thanks to any face creams or skin treatments—what people saw was what they got. Her eyebrows were naturally arched and helped to make her appear much younger than she really was. She had made up her mind when she had accepted her current position that although she would be surrounded by old people, she would not allow herself to look old. She followed fashion trends and would not be seen in anything out-of-style.

When she heard a car door slam, she turned and pushed the slats on the blind aside to get a look at the occupants. Her curiosity about the pair had been tweaked ever since their correspondence indicated, that while they were sisters, they did not want to live together nor did they want to reside in the same wing.

"Well, this will be a new situation for me—that's for sure," Hortense said to herself.

In a few moments, her office door opened and Mary Beth, the receptionist, ushered two elegantly-attired women into the room.

"Welcome," Hortense said enthusiastically, "I'm Hortense Ferndale. I'm so delighted to know you are interested in our facility."

The taller woman moved forward and extended her hand. "Mrs. Ferndale, I am Julia LaPointe and this is my sister, Enid Murphy. By the way, are you by chance related to the Ferndales who are in the furniture business? My late husband and Otto Ferndale were close friends."

Hortense was taken aback. A question about her husband's distant relatives, whom she detested, was certainly not one that she had anticipated. As she busied herself by gathering a few brochures for the sisters, she wrestled with herself about the most appropriate way to answer the question. Finally, she replied, "They are relatives, but I seldom get to see them. Now, you may take these brochures along on the tour. Please feel free to refer to them as you see fit. I thought you would appreciate having them because they'll help you get familiar with the various eating areas, shops, and other types of services you'll have at your fingertips if you choose one of our apartments." Moving from behind her desk, Hortense said, "Marty Miller, one of our most active residents, will be joining us for the tour. I have found most people who are interested in residing here enjoy talking with current residents."

"That will be fine," Julia said as she leaned forward to pick up the brochures. "Enid and I have looked over the materials you mailed to us. We prefer **not** to take up residence in the same wing. We each like our own space. If you cannot meet this requirement, we have no interest in touring the facility."

Hortense glanced at her visitors. Both were tall and slender. She admired their taste in dress, and their hair styles represented the latest cuts. She judged Julia was probably a size four, while Enid was closer to an eight. Hortense sensed immediately that it would be Julia who would have to be convinced to become a resident—Enid simply smiled and nodded her head in agreement. "The good news: I'm able to accommodate both of you. We have one available apartment on Daffodil Lane and another on Lilac Lane. They both have two bedrooms and large walk-in closets. We have a total of six lanes, each one named after a flower, for residents and two lanes to accommodate the restaurants, pools, and meeting rooms. You'll see all of these wonderful places during our tour," Hortense assured the two women.

"I have a question," Enid said almost in a whisper as she removed a pair of glasses from her leather purse. "I'm curious about the cafe called *The Night Owl.*"

"You would ask *that*," Julia chided. "You're not interested in the important components, but you're eager to learn about places to eat," Julia admonished. "Your obsession with food is beginning to show itself on your hips."

Hortense blinked. Julia had just slammed her sister in an insensitive manner. Now Hortense began to doubt whether she could handle the sisters who apparently were not too fond of one another. Enid simply looked past her sister and began drumming her fingers on the table.

"Will you stop that?" Julia asked sharply.

Hortense had to take over the discussion. "You'll find everything here at Morning Glory Hill has been designed to create a safe environment for our residents. From Hannah's Meditation Room, which is a serene sanctuary where residents spend time to unwind and focus on themselves and clear their minds, to the technical room where you will find the latest pieces of technology for your use, to the spa and swimming pool, are all areas where the needs of seniors have been addressed. But, ladies, our residents represent our most outstanding asset. The men and women who reside here have proven to be above reproach. You will find yourselves among people who will contribute to your sense of community and well-being."

"I am impressed," Julia said. "I hope what you say is true."

Hortense breathed a sigh of relief. "After our tour, I have arranged for a small luncheon where you'll meet several other residents."

Julia was the first to stand—indicating that she was ready to move on. Relieved that Marty Miller, a resident since the facility had opened, was waiting to join them, Hortense performed the necessary introductions. "Marty not only serves as the mayor of Lilac Lane, but the apartment next to hers is available."

As they moved down the hallway, Hortense became aware of Julia's unusual walk. She almost chuckled when she realized Julia walked like a llama—head up, chin out a bit, and a look of disdain on her face. As soon as they entered the empty apartment, Julia began opening and closing almost every drawer and door. Enid, on the other hand, seemed to be interested only in the view from the large front window.

"Tell me, Mrs. Miller, what do you like best about Morning Glory Hill?" Enid asked almost shyly.

"That's a hard question to answer. I like everything here. While I certainly miss the beautiful home I had shared with my late husband, I am quite comfortable here. The many conveniences and various activities that we have are greatly appreciated by all of us. And, the fact that we have our own council, where we can meet to share our ideas and our concerns openly with one another, is a huge sense of comfort. We residents lovingly refer to our facility as MGH. And, please call me Marty."

"Let's go over to Daffodil Lane where we have a similar apartment available," Hortense suggested.

"Just a minute," Julia said. "Who was the person who lived here before and why did they leave? I'm particularly interested in whether or not that person had any communicable diseases."

Enid did not try to hide her disgust. "Julia, what a ridiculous question."

"Yes, you would think that," Julia chastised as she turned her back on her sister.

"The woman who lived here was Jesse Yoder, a sweet, retired elementary teacher. She died of a massive heart attack. We miss her dearly. She had an adorable habit of banging her cane on the floor and rhyming at the end of every sentence that she spoke," Hortense explained lightheartedly.

"Adorable? I would call such a habit infantile," Julia replied.

"Julia," Enid murmured. "You have no right to say such a nasty thing."

"If the truth is nasty, so be it. Enid, just be quiet." Julia grumbled as she crossed her arms. "Just to clear up any misconception about why we have decided to look at this place—we each have a son who works for Mainstream Building Supplies on an administrative level. They recommended your facility because they wanted to have us close by. I hope my acquiescence to their request turns out to our advantage."

Marty wanted to turn things around and decided that she would point out some of the features she felt represented the facility and its mission. "This is our lobby, but we affectionately refer to it as *The Square.* As you can see, the carpet has MGH emblazoned in the center. The furniture was created by Kendrick Harrison, award winning designer, and is laid out in such a manner as to encourage small groups to gather and socialize. The marble-topped table holding the hurricane lamp, as well as the occasional chair to the left are all items that belonged to our benefactors. Let me show you the sanctuary," Marty said as she opened the door to *Hannah's Meditation Room."*

"Oh, this *is* relaxing," Julia purred. "I love the water fountain. It's so restful and quiet that I understand why it is considered a sanctuary. Who is Hannah?"

"Hannah Smoker and her husband provided the financing necessary to build this facility. Mrs. Smoker was a gentle woman who realized all of us, from time to time, need a quiet place to go to allow ourselves to regenerate and get in touch with our own souls," Marty explained.

"Am I right that there is no direct religious affiliation in this facility?" Julia asked.

Hortense took a deep breath. "While our founders were Mennonites, you are correct. We are proud to say that our residents represent many faiths. The Smokers were adamant that religion was a personal choice. Residency here is not dependent on where or how one worships. Let's head over to Daffodil Lane."

When they entered the vacant apartment, Julia immediately asked, "And who was the last tenant in this apartment?"

"Colonel Matthew Anderson, a rather distinguished gentleman, lived here for only a few months. He decided that he wanted to be closer to his old friends so he moved to California," Hortense explained.

Marty rolled her eyes.

"Mrs. Miller, you don't agree with Mrs. Ferndale?' Julia asked.

Not wanting to go into a lengthy explanation, Marty said, "He was a bit disagreeable. I hope that he'll be happier in his new residence."

Hortense felt as if this day would never end. As they entered the dining room, she was relieved to hear laughter and chatter among the guests. Perhaps, just perhaps, Julia wouldn't insult anyone else. William Williams and Frank Snyder immediately stood and pulled out chairs for the sisters. Frank, a retired dairy farmer, towered over William as he guided Julia to her seat. Rosebud McClaren, a diminutive attractive woman, and Celeste Mayfair, a chubby, curly-headed woman, welcomed the visitors warmly. In no time at all lively upbeat conversations filled the air.

"I'm curious," Julia said. "Mr. Williams, Hortense mentioned you play the piano. What is your favorite genre?"

"Please, call me William. While my favorite is country-western, I play all types of music," William explained.

"Wait until you hear William and Abigail Becker," Rosebud said eagerly. She then proceeded to tell the newcomers all about the talents of this couple and how the two of them entertain the residents quite frequently.

"It sounds like this is a very active place," Julia said. "While I much prefer classical music, I guess I can get used to the twang-twang of country. Celeste, are you a certified librarian?"

"Unfortunately, no. But I do my best. If there's a book you're interested in, just complete a request form and I'll try to accommodate you. You'll find the forms in any of the book nooks," Celeste explained.

"You may want to consider taking some courses at the local university. You may just find them beneficial." Julia sniffed.

Celeste was mortified. She wanted to lash out at the self-centered Julia, but she bit her lip and kept quiet.

A cone of silence fell over the once-happy diners. The residents exchanged looks with one another and shifted in their seats. The luncheon was over. One by one, they began standing and shaking hands with the prospective guests.

Julia made it known that she was interested in the apartment on Lilac Lane. Enid graciously accepted the one on Daffodil Lane. Now it was Marty's time to feel nervous. This arrogant woman was going to be her neighbor and she had to get along with her. She jumped when Julia turned to her and said, "My dear Marty—may I call you Marty?" Then without waiting for an answer, she added, "You are certainly welcome to come over to my residence anytime as long as you call first. Oh, another consideration—I have a car, Enid does not. Her son wisely took her driver's license away from her some time ago," Julia said smugly.

Hortense was eager to bring this visit to an end. "I'll escort you ladies to your car," she offered as pleasantly as she could.

Marty and Frank watched as the sisters disappeared from view. Frank shook his head, leaned over to Marty and whispered, "I guess Julia can get along very well without any friends at all."

CHAPTER 2

Enid had finally unwrapped her last teapot from the movers' carton—all 32 teapots had arrived and, much to her relief, none had any signs of damage. Each little treasure resurrected memories of how it had landed in her collection. Of course, one special pot had been placed on the center shelf of her china closet. She fondly recalled the day her husband had given it to her—not in a brightly wrapped package, but in a little paper bag that the local five-and-dime had used for the gift he had purchased for their first anniversary. While most of the other pots were more elegantly designed, with some of them edged in gold, none of them were treasured more than this little *Brown Betty* with a tiny chip on it spout. Oh, how she had cried the day that she had bumped her precious gift against the faucet and had watched the little chip disappear down the drain.

Julia could never abide Enid's love of teapots. She refused to acknowledge the significant role they played in society. Enid had tried to explain this to Julia more than once. Enid loved the charm created by the use of teapots—an symbol of genteel times that nowadays seems to have been forgotten.

But, then again, she realized Julia had never found anything she truly treasured.

When her mantel clock struck midnight, she realized she was hungry. Then, she recalled *The Night Owl*. She hurried over to her desk and retrieved the packet of brochures Hortense had given her two weeks ago. She wondered if anyone would really be there. As a little smile crept over her face, with the feeling like she was somehow breaking the rules, she adjusted the sash of her bathrobe securely around her waist, took a quick look at herself in her hallway mirror, pulled a few locks of hair over her forehead to try to cover a wrinkle or two, and headed out the door.

As she entered *The Square,* she almost changed her mind when she didn't see anyone. Suddenly, she became aware of a lamppost with a little, neon owl perched on the top at the entrance to Violet Lane. Well, even if she had to sit by herself, she was determined to complete her little venture. Even from some distance, she could see a lighted bakery case filled with goodies.

Although she spied a pair of legs stretched out, the figure was hidden from her view. She breathed a sigh of relief when she spotted the piano player sitting with another gentleman. "Hello, William," Enid said in a relieved tone.

As William shook her hand, she noticed that his long, slender fingers were strong—she assumed it was the result of all that piano playing. She had been impressed when she had met him during the tour—a tall man with handsome facial features and a smile that could charm the birds out of the trees. .

"Enid, how nice of you to join us. Enid, this fine specimen of a man is Nigel Nuggett, the best dancer in all of Pennsylvania. Nigel, this is Enid Murphy. She and her sister are our new neighbors," William said graciously.

"Julia's not here, yet. She's not moving in until Friday," Enid explained. "She'll be living on the other side of Marty Miller."

"Oh, you won't be living together?" Nigel asked as he adjusted his hands over his substantial girth.

"No. We each like our own space," Enid said quickly.

"I see," Nigel said as he winked his eye.

"Please join us, Enid," William said. "Stretch is the guy in charge of this little place. You can get all kinds of sandwiches and salads. Nigel and I like to hang in here while Stretch is baking cookies and making doughnuts. Oh, and you can get ice cream, too."

"Hot tea and a cookie sound great to me," Enid replied.

"Hey, Stretch, you have a customer," William yelled.

After Stretch had taken her order and disappeared back into the kitchen, Enid said, "My, he's a pleasant person."

"He's not only nice, but he's one hell of a baker, too. He used to be a jockey. We're lucky to have him. Now, Enid, tell us a little something about yourself," William encouraged.

"I was married to Carl, my high school sweetheart just a few months after we graduated. We had just celebrated our fifty-third anniversary when I lost him. I have a son who lives nearby and a daughter who lives in Las Vegas."

"Vegas, wow," Nigel gushed. "I would love to go to Vegas. Maybe you and I could do that some time."

"Enid, don't pay him any attention. Nigel means well," William cautioned.

Enid laughed. "What a nice compliment. It's been a long time since anyone wanted to take a trip with me," she said as she gently tapped Nigel's arm.

"Is your daughter a showgirl?" Nigel asked eagerly.

Enid chuckled. "Oh, my, no," she replied. "Helena's a bit too old for such things. She's in upper management. I think she has something to do with financial planning, or something like that."

"Do you get to see her often?" Nigel asked.

"I haven't been out there for two years. I just can't handle traveling any more. But, she'll be here next month and I can't wait to see her," Enid explained. "Now, Nigel, tell me about your dancing."

"I started dancing when I was a kid. But, when the other kids made fun of me, saying that I looked like a giant toy top, I quit. Later, I took up ballroom dancing and found that I really enjoyed being on the dance floor," Nigel said proudly as his face lit up. "I may be a bit round, but I'm as light as a feather on my feet."

"Enid, he's being modest. I swear he's a better dancer than most of those you see on television. He's especially good when he dances with Rosebud McClaren. I understand that you met her on your tour. She's one of those people who just doesn't seem to age. Remarkably, she also seems to be almost free from pesky senior citizen problems," William asserted.

"Huh, that was before she met her snooty doctor friend… Phillip something-or-other."

"Dandridge—his last name is Dandridge," William reminded Nigel.

"Yeah, yeah. Enid, do you know what lies at the bottom of the ocean and shakes a lot?"

Enid was impressed with Nigel's voice—there was a softness, a feeling of caring, behind his words. When she took notice of the twinkle in Nigel's eyes, she realized that this was a joke. She pretended to think about it for a minute and then said, "Gee, I haven't the foggiest idea."

Nigel leaned back, smiled and then chuckled, "A nervous wreck!"

Enid laughed. "Thank you, Nigel. My first good laugh I had today. By the way, my sister Julia loves to dance—no line dancing and such. I have to admit that she's good on the dance floor. In fact, it's probably the one place where she allows herself to smile. However, she won't like your jokes." She quickly added. "But I do."

"Oh, you'll hear many more, Enid. He has a treasure trove of them stored under that curly hair," William said. "Are you all settled in?"

"Well, almost. I did bring some things here that I should have gotten rid of before I moved," Enid said. "Some dishes and things, and oh, three full-length mirrors."

"Oh, Enid, you naughty girl you," Nigel teased.

Enid looked perplexed.

"There he goes again. You have to learn to ignore Nigel most of the time," William cautioned. "Nigel has a two-track mind—one is dancing and the other is sex. Now, getting back to your unwanted items. We have a room near the deli called *The Exchange Room* where you can place your unwanted dishes and other small things on a table. Residents may leave things they no longer want, or, if they wish, take an item they see on the table they can use. However, we have a storage room in the garage area where residents may place furniture and large items, such as your mirrors, until they decide what they want to do with them."

"What a great idea. Is there a time limit on how long you may keep something in that storage area?" Enid asked.

"I don't think so. Just call the desk and Mary Beth will make the necessary arrangements to have them moved for you," William explained.

"Nigel, I used to make wedding gowns and formal dresses. My husband bought the full-length mirrors at a flea market so I could use them in my sewing room for the ladies to admire the finished products." Enid said with a smile. "Sorry to disappoint you...no sex—just fashion."

"I hope you get involved in some of the activities we have here. You may want to visit Barry Adams, our Activities Director. His office is next to the front desk. You can't miss him. He still continues to dress like the cruise director he was at one time. He's a heck of a nice fellow—always willing to help out and eager to serve," William suggested. "While we don't have a sewing room, we take excursions, attend various classes such as exercise and swimming, and go to ballgames and all kinds of stuff. If you have any suggestions, let Barry know."

"Do you have a chorus?" Enid asked. "I remember hearing about you and Abigail performing musical programs. Is Abigail your wife?"

"She may as well be," Nigel said as he made a face at William.

"Abigail is not my wife. Abigail Becker lives on Marigold Lane, has a beautiful voice, and allows me to accompany her at various times," William explained.

"Oh, come on now, William. We all know you two are an item. Just admit it," Nigel chided.

"Let's ignore him for now, Enid. No, we don't have a chorus, but I think that's a good idea. I'll run it by Abigail and Barry and see what they think. I don't know why we didn't think of that a long time ago," William said, obviously intrigued by the idea. "Thanks for mentioning it."

"William, I apologize for my presumption. Julia would be appalled at my lack of manners," Enid said apologetically.

"No offense taken, my dear," William said gracefully. "I really thank you for asking since I think it would be wonderful to create a choral group."

"I almost didn't come tonight. I didn't know if any women ever came here," Enid mumbled.

"Jessie used to come here all the time. She would amuse us with her little rhymes—used to be a pre-school teacher, I think. Well, anyway, she would bang her cane on the floor a lot. Nigel didn't care for that, but he did like her rhymes. A nice lady. She passed in her sleep," William said. "If I could choose my passing, that's the way I would want to go," William said.

Later, as Enid walked back to her apartment, she was thankful that she had gone to *The Night Owl*. If her experience tonight was any indication of whether or not she would feel at home at MGH, she knew she would. She made two new friends tonight—one, a talented musician and the other a lovable jokester. However, she wasn't going to tell her sister anything about her little escapade—she loved keeping secrets from Julia.

CHAPTER 3

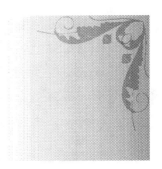

Marty heard the noise of the moving truck and immediately went to the window. She saw Julia get out of her car and walk over to the driver. A small cadre of other people seemed to be directing the movers where to take each piece of furniture as they referred to a schematic that had been spread out on the hood of the truck. Marty was impressed. Julia was going to be an interesting neighbor. If she directed everything like this, who knew what would happen here at MGH in the future.

As she parted her curtains a bit, Marty began feeling guilty about snooping on her new neighbor but she just couldn't pull herself away. She was surprised that Enid was not helping her sister move. Perhaps the chasm between the two women is worse than she had realized. She was pleased when Harvey and Harry Hamilton approached Julia and began a conversation. Knowing how kind and polite they were, Marty knew that they were welcoming her in a gracious manner. After they chatted with Julia for a few minutes, the two of them walked away, holding hands. Marty didn't miss the slight scowl that came over Julia's face as she watched the handsome couple head down the walkway.

When the moving truck had left the parking lot, Marty decided to pay a quick visit to her new neighbor. Picking up the little bouquet of pink roses she had purchased earlier in the day, she headed out the door. As she rang Julia's doorbell, she heard a voice behind her.

"Hello, Marty. Nice to see you again," Enid said as she touched Marty's arm.

Just then Julia opened the door. She smiled when she spotted the roses. "Hello, Marty."

As Marty handed her the small bouquet, she said, "Just a little token to welcome you to MGH."

"Thank you." Julia said as she took the flowers from Marty. Then, turning abruptly towards Enid, she said with a sigh, "Glad you could make it. We're just about finished. Your timing was perfect as usual," Julia said.

Marty felt uncomfortable. "Julia, let me know if you need anything. I know you have lots to do, so I won't hold you up."

Scurrying across *The Square,* Marty headed to the rear of the dining room to attend the monthly *Food for Thought* committee meeting. This small group of five was charged with bringing resident's suggestions, compliments, and complains to Rebecca Hunter, the manager of all the food areas. While Marty was used to serving with Rosebud and Frank on various committees, her only involvement with Samuel had been through the Mayors Council. Hortense had chosen the members so there wasn't too much Marty could do about Samuel's presence. The man gave her the creeps. Samuel was a misogynist, something she would have to learn to deal with. He had a slight hunch in his shoulders that only seemed to make his large hooked nose look even more threatening. His little, black, beady eyes always seemed to be searching for something. What she hated the most about the man was his vain attempts to placate women by ignoring anything they said. She would not be surprised if Rosebud stood up to him—she was tiny, but mighty. Frank, ah Frank, was another matter. The two of them had grown close, very close. She would lean back and just let Frank handle any nonsense that Samuel might generate. Marty was the last of the committee to arrive, so she took her seat quickly and said, "Sorry I'm late. I was welcoming my new neighbor, Julia LaPointe, to MGH."

Ellie May smiled broadly. "From what I hear, you're going to need all your finesse just to remain friends with her. I heard she's a spitfire."

Rebecca laughed, "While I used to handle brash behavior when I was in charge of the mess hall at Fort Lee, I cannot apply the same strategies here," she said lightly.

"I didn't know that you had been in the service, Rebecca. I'm curious. What made you join?" Frank asked.

"Well, I just wanted to get away from the area. My mom had remarried and things were not very pleasant at home so I took the bull by the horns and followed the lead of my brothers and joined the army. I took some tests and, before I knew it, I was sent to Quatermaster School. That was a blessing. I discovered that I enjoyed cooking and, next thing you know, I was in charge of the mess hall," Rebecca said.

"I'm impressed," Samuel Long grumbled. "Most women would not have the fortitude nor the backbone to take on an assignment like that. This job is probably not as challenging as working for the army. I must confess, however, I still believe that we should not have women in the service. They are too fragile. Women cannot handle stress. As men, it is our duty to protect our women."

Rebecca didn't want to start an argument with Samuel so she pretended that she hadn't heard what he had said. She looked at his pathetic frame and realized she could put him down on his knees in a split second. "Actually, I enjoy my position here. While it's certainly different from what I faced in the service, it is more rewarding. For instance, I'm pleased to report that Stretch is being promoted. He'll be my assistant as soon as I can get a replacement for him as head baker and manager of *The Night Owl*. Next week, we'll have two new waitresses joining our staff in the dining room and they'll alternate weekends—thus relieving the backup that sometimes occurs in getting everyone served promptly." Rebecca paused, sat back in her chair, and hesitantly said, "Now…I have something to share with you that I am asking you not to take beyond this committee."

"Oh, what happens in this committee, stays in this committee," Rosebud said quietly as she winked at Frank.

"You've got it," Rebecca affirmed. "I can't be certain of this, but *someone* may be stealing our cloth napkins."

The committee members looked at one another as if they were not sure that they had heard Rebecca correctly.

"I know this sounds strange, but I think that someone is pilfering the pink, the white and the gray table napkins.

21

I know, folks…I know. Why would anyone want them?" Putting her hands in the air, to gesture that she was as puzzled as they were, she then stated, "I have checked with the laundry and they don't have any napkins lying around anywhere, and I've taken the inventory three times myself just to be certain that the count is accurate. So far we've lost a total of 12 white, 6 gray, and 18 pink napkins—not monumental, but, if this continues, it will impact our budget in a negative manner."

"Now, just a minute," Samuel challenged. "Unless someone is planning on opening a linen shop, why would they do that? How about the other napkins…like the black, green, and purple ones?" Samuel questioned.

"Those stand at full count. Just the pink, white and gray ones seem to be disappearing," Rebecca stated.

"Are you certain that they're not being stored somewhere else?" Samuel asked.

"Maybe we need to stand guard at the doorway each night and frisk everyone," Ellie May jested.

"You cannot be serious, my dear woman, or has your love of crime stories run amuck?" Samuel said in an annoying manner.

"Do you have a better idea, Mr. Mayor?" Ellie May replied haughtily.

"Maybe we could have the wait staff check each table after the residents leave their tables. I'm not certain that there's another way to keep track of the napkins," Rosebud offered.

"But, if the napkin thief steals one from a table other than the one he is sitting at, we won't be able to trace it to any one person," Marty reasoned.

"Wait a minute, folks, do you realize how absurd this conversation is?" Frank asked.

"I agree, but I thought the committee should know. For now, just keep your eyes open, and if you see anything that may shed light on this problem, please contact me," Rebecca suggested. "Does anyone have any questions for me regarding the food?" Rebecca asked.

"I do," Rosebud said. "I want to congratulate Stretch on his latest batch of peanut butter cookies. They were almost as good as the ones Ellie May makes."

"I don't like to complain, Rebecca, but…"

"Hold it, Frank, I don't consider the suggestions and concerns of the residents as *complaints*. If I'm not aware of any problems, how can I improve on our service?" Rebecca remarked.

"Well, it's the mashed potatoes. They are frequently lumpy and always taste bland," Frank said rather hesitantly. "Here in PA we love our mashed potatoes, but they need to have milk, butter and salt in them."

"I've been thinking of serving two kinds of mashed potatoes…one that has salt and butter….and one that doesn't," Rebecca suggested.

"That sounds like a lot of extra work for you, Rebecca," Frank reasoned.

"Our kitchen help will have to make certain that they know which is which…we have lots of people here who are on salt restricted diets. Maybe I'll try it to see if it's well-received," Rebecca offered. "Anything else?"

Samuel practically ran out the doorway, almost knocking Ellie May off her feet. He said something under his breath, but he just kept moving.

As the rest of them walked down the hallway together, Frank said, "You can tell that Rebecca was in the service by two things: first, her posture is perfect, and second, she's well organized."

Rubbing her hands together, Ellie May rationalized, "That may well be, but I'm delighted that we have a napkin thief. Now we have another crime to solve. I know this can't compare to the time we tracked down that fornicating couple last year, but it will have to do. Every time I think of old man Knoblauch with a feather boa wrapped around his bony, ugly body as he watched a naked floozy woman dance all over the place, I break out laughing. Catching someone who's stealing napkins can't compare to a racy caper. But, we need to solve this before all the napkins disappear. After all, a good detective must solve all types of mysteries. And, after all, a minor case is better than no case at all.

CHAPTER 4

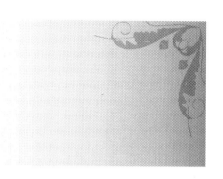

Ellie May had just finished running the carpet sweeper. She stepped back to inspect what she had accomplished. She could never understand how just one person and a little dog could create such clutter. Ellie May was an excellent housekeeper. Her friends Rosebud and Marty always said that they could eat off her floors since they were so clean. While her life used to revolve around taking care of others, it now focused on her two friends and her detective shows, especially *True Detective*. The thought of trying to solve *The Case of the Purloined Dinner Napkins* made her smile. Even seasoned detectives had to start somewhere. And, this case was enticing enough to kick her investigative juices into overdrive.

She pulled off the bandana from around her head and shook her wavy hair from side to side. Ellie May had one glowing feature to help soften her plain face—natural wavy hair. She was immensely proud of her hair. And, when the weather was humid, and her friends were dealing with frizzy hair, she just quietly enjoyed how they envied her waves. After all, something's better than nothing.

Pulling up her antique desk chair to her desk, she tapped her front tooth with her pen and began to ponder ways to discover who was stealing napkins from the dining room. While she couldn't really call this a *caper*, it was a mystery and that made her happy. She decided to make a list of the steps involved in solving the crime. She wanted to handle the case by herself, so she needed to be as professional as possible. Of course, it would be great if she could catch the thief in the act. That would require her to watch as many diners as possible, especially when they were leaving their tables. She closed her eyes as she pictured the dining room. When the thief stood up, perhaps he already had put the napkin in his pocket. Then she remembered some women brought purses with them ino the dining room—another way to get ill-gotten gain out of the room.

Ellie May listed the laundry room next. Maybe it was a worker who was taking the napkins. She needed to gain access to that room. Ellie May was aware that the laundry room was downstairs, that there was only one elevator to the basement and that a key was needed to make it work. Getting a key would take a bit more ingenuity.

She intended to keep her plans from Marty and Rosebud until she needed help. She really wanted to solve the crime without help. After all, even Sherlock Holmes didn't tell Dr. Watson everything—he always remained the lead detective. Her new motto from now on would be: *I've got to do what I have to do in order to do what I want to do!*

CHAPTER 5

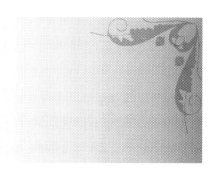

E nid was sitting on a sofa in *The Square* eagerly reading the latest MGH newsletter. There was much she wanted to learn about this fascinating place that she now called *home*. She was so immersed in reading that she failed to notice when Harvey Hamilton sat down beside her.

"Hello, Miss Enid," Harvey said when he realized she became aware of him.

"Mr. Hamilton, hello," Enid said politely.

"Just call me Harvey. Harry and I met you the other day outside Marty's apartment."

"Certainly. I just can't get over how nice everyone is here. I'm so pleased that I chose this facility. How long have you resided here, Harvey?"

"Well, let's see. Harry and I moved in about a year and a half ago. But, really I feel that we've been here much longer than that. Have you settled in yet?" Harvey inquired.

"Just about. Harvey, can you tell me more about the *Harvest Moon Bazaar*?" Enid asked. "I was reading about it in this newsletter. I believe that residents are being asked to make something to help support The Children's Hospital Benefit Fund."

"This event is being sponsored by three retirement facilities. One, of course, is our own MGH, Johnson's Independent Living is another, and the third is the new Evergreen Glen. Residents of these facilities are encouraged to make items that can be purchased by the general public. However, the kicker here is that all the money taken in goes to the charity. For instance, Frank will probably be making a dollhouse, Ellie May will no doubt be baking for days, and Samuel will probably be doing something involving local history. Does that help?" Harvey asked.

"I'm afraid not. I'm what's known as *artistically challenged*," Enid said as she smiled shyly. "I'd like to help, but I don't know what I can do."

"How about hobbies? Anything like that interest you?"

"Enid chuckled. "You won't believe this, but I collect teapots."

"Fascinating," Harvey said. "Tell me more about your collection."

"Well, it began when my husband gave me a pretty little teapot called a *Brown Betty* on our first wedding anniversary. It grew from then on. I have all kinds of teapots—most are china, but I have one in cast iron. Some have intricate designs, like a Sadler English Teapot with a scene from *A Christmas Carol* painted on it. I also have one from *The Wizard of Oz* and I have a unique one shaped like a rabbit," Enid rattled on, obviously enjoying talking about her prized collection.

"Hmm...let me think about that for a moment. Teapots...hmm. Interesting. Makes one think of elegant times. I got it! Why don't you create a little booklet about teapots? And—oh, I can get Harry to take photos. What do you think about that?" Harvey asked eagerly. "Harry's a professional photographer—won prizes and such for his work. That large photo of a cat over there above the reception desk is just one of his award-winning works. By the way, the cat's name is Oscar and he's Samuel's prized possession."

"Do you really think anyone would be interested in my teapots?" Enid asked in amazement.

"You could also expand on your theme by providing information about various types of teas—like where they are grown and how they are best served," Harvey went on eagerly.

"While I can type, I don't know how to use a computer," Enid said apprehensively.

"I can help with that part. Enid, this could be the hit of the event. Look, you could offer a free cup of tea to everyone who purchases a book. Or, maybe you could offer several samples for tasting. You could put wrought iron chairs around matching tables with little lace doilies on them— just like an open invitation for people to sit down and sip tea, poured from your prized teapots."

Enid was pleased that Harvey was genuinely excited about the whole concept. And, to be honest, so was she. "Harvey, Marty showed me photos of some of the events held here last year where you served as the decorator and your ideas were fabulous. Tell me more about your background," Enid said excitedly.

"I was an event planner. I had my own company and, along with a staff of ten, I decorated rooms, auditoriums, warehouses and buildings of all shapes and sizes for corporate events and for large, up-scale private parties, weddings, graduations, bar mitzvahs, anniversaries—you name it. All of this was hard to give up, but for the sake of our retirement, I did. Harry and I agreed that we each would only use our expertise on a part-time basis. This would be something the three of us could work on together. You must realize that it will take some work, but we have six months to prepare. What do you say, Enid?"

"You'll have to keep me on task, Harvey. As my sister often reminds me, I can be a bit on the lazy side. How do I get started?" an eager Enid asked.

"Make a list of the teapots and then we'll meet with Harry to set up a schedule for the photos. When you identify the ones you want to include in the book, you can begin your research. You'll probably have some that may need several paragraphs to describe, while others may be covered in just several sentences. You can probably use the same method to select which teas you want to include. If you'd like, I could help you plan the layout of the book and give you some suggestions for a cover. Meanwhile, I'll look around for the right tables and chairs," Harvey expounded as he stood. "Enid, you made my day. I haven't felt this excited about a project in a long time."

"Harvey, I have one favor to ask. Can we keep this between us? I'd rather not have to listen to my sister tell me why this is a dumb idea," Enid murmured as she took Harvey's hand.

"You got it, Enid. Mums the word!"

CHAPTER 6

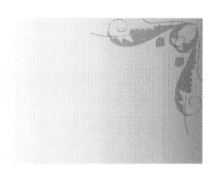

Samuel was hurrying across *The Square* on his way to conduct the monthly MGH Mayors Council meeting. He was not himself today. In fact, he almost canceled the meeting because of his vertigo problem. It irritated him that he would be bothered with what he felt was a *woman's problem.* He rationalized that a man of his stature was superior in both mind and body, and that he should be free from such a problem. He had been everywhere. He had consulted with everyone. He had tried all kinds of treatmens—nothing.

He wasn't surprised to see that Sally Fisher, mayor of Marigold Lane, was already there. She was always the first one to show up for anything—especially when food was being served. But, when he discovered several other residents were also seated in the meeting room, his displeasure grew stronger. He didn't even try to hide his annoyance. Samuel just didn't like it when everything was not going his way. It was bad enough that that twit, Harry Hamilton, had been leading him around by the nose for some time. How much more must he tolerate? If only he hadn't gotten caught by Harry's security camera when he was peering in their front window that dreadful night, things would be radically different. That damned Harry and his prize-winning photo of his cat, Oscar, only added fuel to the fire. Although Harry had never challenged him directly about his *peeping Tom episode*, he could sense Harry *knew* that Samuel *knew* that he *knew* he had been caught. Harry had never told him directly he really had a photo—Samuel surmised it just by Harry's demeanor. No wonder he had vertigo. It was all Harry's fault.

"Good morning, Samuel," Marty said cheerfully.

Samuel looked at her briefly, turned his head towards Celeste Mayfair, mayor of Petunia, who was filing in, and just mumbled something unintelligible.

It wasn't long before all six mayors were seated at the head table. Samuel rapped his gavel sharply, scaring Rosebud, a regular attendee. "My goodness, Samuel, you frightened me," Rosebud said, obviously annoyed.

Without apologizing, Samuel ordered, "Let's get started. Marty, you have the first item," Samuel rattled off as he flipped through his paperwork noisily. He never noticed that Harry Hamilton had slipped quietly into the room, taking a seat in the back row.

"Remember, tomorrow afternoon we'll host a reception for our newest residents—Julia LaPointe and her sister Enid Murphy. Julia is my neighbor and Enid lives on Daffodil and is a neighbor of Catherine Blessing, whom we honored just last month when she moved in. I hope you'll take the time to introduce yourselves to these ladies and make them feel welcome. It's so nice to have all our apartments occupied again," Marty said encouragingly.

Just as Samuel was getting ready to move to the next agenda item, Ellie May interrupted, "You know, I haven't seen Catherine in the dining room at all. I'm a bit worried about her. Marty, I assume you paid her a welcome visit with your basket of goodies and things. Did she express any qualms about socializing with the rest of us?"

"Catherine has joined the book club, but she's a very private person and is content to spend considerable time in her apartment. I feel that she'll join us in other activities before too long," Marty explained. "She's still getting used to her wheelchair."

"Ladies, please hold your gossip session after the meeting. Now, Frank, you have Item 2," Samuel directed sharply.

"Good news for those woodworkers who live here. The woodshop is now equipped with some of the latest power tools to help us make professional-looking items. However, everyone first must take a course in operating the equipment. And, before using the equipment, you must check in with Preston, the head of our maintenance crew. Interested parties, men or women, may sign up for classes at the front desk," Frank explained.

"Really?" Samuel bristled. "You fully intend to allow women to use power equipment?" Samuel raised his eyebrows and squinted his eyes so hard that they seemed to disappear into his head.

"Everyone will be tested by a representative from Ziegler and Company, the donors of all this equipment," Frank said evenly.

Some spectators began discussing how they could take advantage of the new power tools. Samuel was obviously annoyed. He rapped the gavel again, shifted in his seat and sighed heavily.

"I guess by now all of you have heard about the incident that occurred at the Johnson Independent Living facility," Samuel growled mechanically.

"No," Rosebud purred. "What happened?"

"Someone found a resident fob and used it to drive a car into their garage. Apparently, when a lady drove into the garage a few minutes later, she was robbed," Samuel exclaimed.

"Goodness gracious," Rosebud sighed as she put her hand over her mouth. "I hope she wasn't hurt." Rosebud reached up to check on the small tiara that was nestled in her hair.

"She's fine. Now, as I tried to tell you before I was interrupted, as a result, that facility has installed a camera to take pictures of the people using their fobs. We'll all be getting a ballot to vote whether or not we want a similar mechanism installed at our garage. While administration supports the use of cameras, I strongly encourage all of you to carefully consider this privacy infringement before you vote. I am sick and tired of seeing cameras everywhere I look," Samuel barked. "I wholeheartedly suggest you vote against cameras. These women need to take care of themselves and stop whining."

"Surely you don't mean that," Frank demurred.

"Yes, I do. Residents need to understand what responsibility is. They're entrusted with a fob, so they need to protect it. They certainly wouldn't let the doors of their apartments unlocked," Samuel said as he rifled through his papers. After he let everyone know he was thoroughly annoyed, Samuel went through the other agenda items quite rapidly. He then quickly brought the meeting to an end. He stacked his papers, stood up and stormed out of the meeting room.

"What was *that* all about?" Rosebud asked.

"I'm not sure," Frank answered. "Perhaps Samuel wasn't feeling well. You know how private he is about such matters. I don't think he intended to be rude."

"Well, he was," Rosebud declared. "I'm not a mayor, only a resident, but I won't put up with such rude treatment again. I can't blame him for not wanting his picture taken— that grumpy-looking, wrinkled face of his would probably break the camera."

"I'm glad that none of the new residents were in attendance today," Celeste added. "They might be afraid to ever come back."

Just then, Harry, who had been sitting quietly in the back row, said, "Samuel may be having a difficult time with his conscience."

"Meaning what?" Frank quizzed.

"Nothing in particular," Harry chirped as he smiled broadly. "But he does seem to act like a man who is fighting off demons."

CHAPTER 7

Marty was rearranging her doll collection. Her great-granddaughter and she had been playing with them all afternoon. Little Gretchen loved to take the dolls out of the case, bestow kisses, and put them back in different places. Marty went right along with the flow. But, as soon as Gretchen and her mother left the apartment, she put each doll back on its original shelf. Ever since the time Gretchen had removed a necklace from one doll and had placed it around a teddy bear's neck and had put him in a secret hiding place, Marty wanted to be certain all the dolls were there—in their assigned spots. Someday, if Julia ever became a bit more pleasant, she would invite her new neighbor over for tea and then show off her prized collection.

A small group would be gathering tonight for dinner in the main dining room to celebrate Rosebud's 70th birthday. Ellie May was baking Rosebud's favorite cake and Frank was bringing a bouquet of roses. As a surprise, Marty had invited Phillip Dandridge, the retired doctor who Rosebud had been seeing for the past few months, to also join them. Checking the clock, she hurriedly showered and dressed.

She no sooner laid her hairbrush down when the phone rang.

"Are you ready?" Ellie May asked anxiously.

"Sure. Do you need help with the cake?" Marty asked.

"No, I just want us to be down there before Rosebud gets there. You know, so we can surprise her," Ellie May explained. "I'm glad Phillip is coming. Oh, I think he's so handsome, don't you? Ever since the two of them went to Vegas together, they've been thick as thieves."

Marty laughed. "He's a good match for Rosebud. I'll see you there."

As Marty began to think about Rosebud and Phillip, her thoughts shifted to Frank. Ever since they went to the prom last summer, Frank and Marty could also be considered a couple. Now, Marty could not imagine her life without Frank. She never dreamed she would fall in love at her age. Love, she had always thought, was for the young. But, she was in love. She felt blessed that she had met Frank and had been lucky enough to spend so much time with him—she was afraid to wish for more. She wasn't certain he would want any more than they already had. Pulling herself out of her daydreams of Frank, she hurried down the lane to Rosebud's party.

Ellie May had positioned the cake in the center of the dining room table and had placed little party favors beside each sparkling white napkin—immediately her antenna went up—white, the kind the napkin thief steals. This could be the day she captures the criminal. She needed to be alert. The thief had been clever enough to evade being caught in the act, so far. However, Ellie May was determined to be just as clever as that rascal.

The guests had all arrived a few minutes before Rosebud sashayed in the door. She certainly did not look her age. Wearing a gray satin blouse, ruched on the sides, along with a pencil-slim, black silk skirt, she was the epitome of elegance. Sometimes Rosebud would wear strange combinations when she dressed and it wasn't unusual to see her in short skirts and fish-net stockings—but not tonight. She looked as if she had stepped out of an ad in *Elle*. Phillip immediately went to her side and escorted her to the table. He leaned over and whispered something into her ear. Rosebud was enthralled. She beamed.

"Happy birthday," Frank said as he handed her the roses.

"Thank you, Frank. How thoughtful. This is so nice of all of you. I must say that you've made me very happy."

All during dinner, Ellie May's eyes were constantly scanning the crowd. She had identified several diners who could possibly be *people of interest*. However, when she spotted a lady with an open tote bag by her side, leaning down as if she were putting something in the bag, her attention immediately focused only on her. Ellie May could see something white protruding from the bag. She needed to get closer to her suspect. Getting up from the table, Ellie May excused herself and headed towards that tote bag, hoping all the while she could pull this caper off. When she was alongside the bag, she used her foot to push the bag over, spilling the contents onto the floor,

"Oh," Ellie May purred, acting surprised, "I'm so sorry. Please let me help you," she mumbled as the woman started to gather her belongings. As Ellie May reached for the white item, she fully expected to find a dinner napkin, only to be totally mortified to discover she was clutching a Depends. Hoping that no one else saw it, Ellie May pushed it back into the bag as quickly as she could. Looking up at the embarrassed owner, Ellie May began to apologize profusely.

"Are you okay?" the woman asked Ellie May.

Now, totally ashamed of herself, Ellie May assured the lady that she was fine and scurried back to her table.

"Ellie May, what happened over there?" Marty asked innocently.

"Gee, I'm not sure," Ellie May answered sheepishly. "I just stumbled."

"Okay, folks. Let's head over to my apartment where drinks await our arrival," Marty announced. She would question Ellie May later. She certainly didn't buy that *stumble* excuse. Maybe it had to do with Ellie May's obsession with the *napkin thief. How*, Marty had no idea but she wouldn't be surprised if it did.

CHAPTER 8

Marty hadn't slept well. Her scary experience last night was probably the culprit. When she had received a call that her late husband's favorite cousin, Jonathan, had been in an accident and was in grave condition, she knew she had to hurry to his side. Sitting by someone's bedside was always difficult, but when there's a possibility the patient might not pull through, it was hard on the nerves as well as the heartstrings. She stayed there for hours and refused to leave until the doctor assured her that Jonathan had turned the corner and was no longer considered critical.

As she drove out of the hospital parking lot, her apprehension grew. She was not used to driving at night any more. The headlights of the few oncoming cars looked more like starbursts than lights. The streets were deserted—making Marty even more nervous. She wished Frank was seated by her side. Marty had arrived back at MGH a little before three. She couldn't help but think about the incident at the Johnson Independent Living Facility where someone had claimed to have been robbed in the garage. She thought about calling Frank and asking him to come down to the garage, but she couldn't disturb him just because she had herself worked into a frenzy. As she used her fob to get the garage door open, she looked around furtively. When she drove into the building, Marty swore she saw a figure moving in between the cars. Her heart skipped a beat. Pulling herself together, she opened her car door with her shaking hands and moved quickly to the elevator, all the while clutching her cell phone.

Now, in the morning light, she felt like a fool. Before she even stepped into the shower, she called the hospital and was relieved when the nurse informed her that Jonathan was doing very well. She then called the florist and ordered a potted plant with fresh flowers to be delivered to his room.

She chuckled when she thought about the many times when she had been out at all hours of the night without a thought about her safety. Oh, but that was so long ago! What an old worry wart she turned out to be. Just to be safe though, maybe she should report what she thought she had seen in the garage to someone. As she headed to *The Square*, she spotted Samuel.

"Samuel, do you have a few minutes?" Marty asked.

"Certainly, Marty. How may I help you?" he said in a surprisingly civil tone.

Marty explained what had happened in the garage and Samuel listened patiently. "Samuel, I can't be certain that I saw anyone, but in my gut I felt that I did."

Samuel paused for a minute. He didn't want *anyone* investigating *anything* in the garage. He knew that he had to placate Marty so she wouldn't run to Hortense. "I understand what happened. You had had a rough night at the hospital and it was extremely late when you got home.

You were tired and drained and it was only natural that you thought about the Johnson thing. Let me tell you what I found out about that—there was some hanky-panky going on and the fob was never lost. There was no robbery. I understand that that woman has already moved out of the facility—with her husband's blessing, of course. See how things get blown out of proportion? Now, don't you worry your pretty head about that any longer," Samuel said as if he really meant to ease her mind.

"I'm glad to hear there was no robbery. I'm so relieved, Samuel. We can always depend on you to get at the truth. I feel silly now," Marty said.

"No, don't feel that way. I'm glad you told me about it. But, I can **assure** you that, if anyone was in the garage, it was most likely a resident—nothing to be afraid of. I'm off to see Hortense about another matter. I will relay your story to her. I certainly don't want cameras placed at our garage entrance. We have cameras everywhere nowadays. I resent that. One invasion of privacy after another," Samuel said firmly. "We must stand up for our rights. We are adults here and we should be able to come and go without having our pictures taken. You can pay me back by voting against the installation of cameras. As adults, we should be able to do what we want."

As Samuel walked away, with his words still ringing in her ears, Marty couldn't believe how upset he appeared about the cameras. Now Marty began to wonder if the story he had told her was true. He never had looked at her while he was talking—a sure sign, Marty thought— his tale did not ring true.

CHAPTER 9

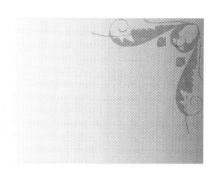

It was a warm early March morning, a precursor to spring. Marty and her two best friends were taking advantage of the warm day as they relaxed in the gazebo on the back lawn of MGH. A small rabbit hopped toward the gazebo and then made a quick escape to the open lawn. Birds were flying from tree to tree, chirping as if they too were heralding the oncoming spring Tiny green sprouts were visible all along the flower bed. While the sun was warm, there was a slight cool breeze moving through the trees.

Ellie May had a light-weight, crocheted shawl wrapped around her shoulders. "Aren't you two chilly?" she asked.

"Not me," Rosebud replied.

"I'm fine," Marty added, but she appeared to be drifting away from their conversation.

It was quiet for a few minutes. "Oh, look…there's another rabbit. How cute," Rosebud said.

"Guess he's practicing for Easter," Ellie May said.

They sat for a few minutes, seemingly enjoying the beauty before their eyes. Marty cleared her throat and sighed. "What's wrong, Marty? You seem preoccupied," a concerned Rosebud asked.

"I guess I should share this with you two. The other night, when I came home from the hospital early in the morning, I was a bit apprehensive about driving into the garage—particularly since we had heard about the robbery over at Johnson's. As I pulled into my parking space, I could have sworn that I saw someone ducking in between the cars. It really shook me up. I could have called Frank on my cell phone to ask him to come down to meet me, but I just didn't want to disturb him if it was only my imagination. I got home safely but I was shaking like a leaf," Marty related. "Later, I had an opportunity to speak with Samuel about it and he was less than helpful. He gave me a lecture and almost insisted that I vote against getting cameras in the garage. He also said that the original story of a robbery was not true and that it was only some hanky-panky going on and I should forget about it," Marty said as she looked for support from her friends.

"While there is one streetlight near our garage, it's still very dark in that corner. I can understand how you must have felt. Samuel seems to be turning into a grouch. I met him on Lilac Lane the other day and he just looked right past me," Rosebud said. "I was annoyed at the snub."

"I for one will vote for cameras," Ellie May said. "If they increase our safety, I'm all for it. Marty, I can understand why you were scared. The garage is a bit creepy, especially when it's late at night, but you should have stayed in your car and called Frank. He would have been there in a heartbeat."

"Samuel did say that he would speak with Hortense. I have to give him that much. Oh, look, here comes Abigail. Let's keep the garage incident to ourselves. I don't want everyone to know how childish I acted," Marty said.

They watched as Abigail, looking as elegant as ever, came across the lawn and up the path leading to the newly-painted gazebo. She always appeared to be gliding rather than walking. Marty's mind went back to the time when she and her friends had decided to try to hook-up Abigail with William to cure her haughtiness. However, the Abigail that was moving so gracefully across the lawn now was a far cry from the one they had first met last year. At that time, she was known to insult just about everyone. And, when they found out about all the charitable work Abigail had been doing at the elementary school, they were shocked. But their plan, called *Operation Smile*, had worked and Abigail and William were a happy couple ever since.

"Hello, everyone. Out enjoying the sun?" Abigail asked.

"We love to come out here to solve the problems of the world," Marty said, as she moved over on the bench to make room for Abigail.

"I just came from a meeting with Barry and Hortense. William and I have been given permission to begin a chorus. We'll be meeting in Room C every Wednesday morning at ten. William will be our director. Now, can we count on you women to join us?" Abigail inquired.

"You certainly don't want me, Abigail. When I sing, I can clear out a room in a hurry," Marty said laughingly.

"You need Ellie May," Rosebud interjected. "She has a lovely alto voice."

"I think the word *lovely* is a bit much," Ellie May said, bashfully. "But I would love to join the chorus. You can count on me."

"Fine. I'll look for you this coming Wednesday. While I'm here, I also want to invite all of you to help with my Easter egg hunt. The students from the elementary school orchestra—you know, they played for us last September—will be presenting another concert for us in three weeks. As a reward for their playing, we could hold a little egg hunt for them. It would be a wonderful surprise," Abigail said hopefully.

"Of course, we'll help," Rosebud said eagerly. "Are you going to use real eggs or those plastic ones?"

"I thought the plastic ones, filled with little candies, would be best for the hunt. I also want to make up little baskets for the children with some real eggs and chocolate bunnies," Abigail explained. "I'll order all the supplies we'll need. I certainly will appreciate extra hands to color the eggs and make up the baskets."

"Sounds delightful!" Rosebud said. "Don't forget the jellybeans! When I was a kid, I used to take all the black jellybeans out of my sisters' Easter baskets. I tried to deny it when my mom questioned me, but my black teeth gave me away." When she stopped laughing, she said, "I'm willing to help in any way that I can. How about you two?" she asked as she glanced at her friends.

"No wonder those children adore you, Abigail. You're such a generous person," Marty said. "Of course, I'll help, too. I enjoyed being with them when they played for us last year. I remember how excited they got whenever they were near you. Abigail, you have done such marvelous work, helping the children purchase instruments. The least I can do is help dye eggs."

"I love coloring eggs," Ellie May said. "I remember when I was little I used to dip the eggs in mugs that my mom had filled with water and those little capsules of dye. We used a little wire dipper, trying very hard not to crack any of the eggs as we turned their shells into bright colors."

"My sister-in-law, who's Greek, dyes her eggs with onion skins and vinegar and serves them with a braided loaf of bread called *tsoureki,*: Rosebud said.

"One time, I had written my girlfriend's name on an egg with a crayon before I colored it a beautiful shade of pink. I couldn't wait until I gave it to her. But she handed me a Ukrainian Easter egg—an intricately designed egg that looked like a stained glass window," Marty said. "I started to cry. I was embarrassed that my egg was just plain pink. But my friend's mom said that my egg was very special because it was *personalized.* I wasn't sure what that meant at the time. When she told me that my friend could eat the egg I gave her, but I could only use the one she gave me for decoration, I stopped crying. For a long time, I thought they had used some kind of magic to get the egg out of the shell without breaking it," Marty said as her shoulders shook as she laughed.

Abigail smiled. "You won't believe this, but I took lessons on how to create Ukrainian Easter eggs. The instructor was a retired army sergeant—a surprisingly versatile lady, who had the patience of Job. It's a multiple step process. Marty, they don't hard boil their eggs. First, a pattern is drawn on a raw egg. Wax is then applied to the lines. The egg is dipped into the lightest colors first. This process is repeated, color after color, until the entire egg is colored. All the wax must now be removed. At this point, the egg is still not finished."

"Shucks, no magic?" Marty asked.

Abigail laughed. "No magic. Now, the egg is coated with polyethylene to make it hard. The contents of the egg must be removed. So, a tiny hole is made in the bottom of the egg, and a fine wire is then inserted into the egg to break the yolk. By holding the egg up and using a tiny plunger, all the contents are blown out of the egg. So, what you have is a beautiful shell without an egg. Ukrainians love to use these eggs to decorate their homes."

"I never knew all of that," Ellie May said. "The process sounds too difficult for me. I think I'll stick to baking cookies."

"It was a bit difficult, but our instructor kept us on-task by reminding us that the decorative shell of a Ukrainian egg is a miracle of beauty and is immersed in religious beliefs, like protecting households and blessing people with good health. One egg we made had triangular shapes all around the shell which she said represented the Trinity. I remember one of the students claimed her aunt, who had been barren, created an egg and then became fertile."

Ellie May's eyes widened. "Really?"

"I can't be sure of that, but the woman claimed that it was true," Abigail replied.

"Stranger things have happened. But I better not take those lessons since I'm a bit too old to become fertile," Rosebud said as she giggled.

"There are so many interesting traditions involving Easter eggs—many that are tightly interwoven with religious beliefs. I do know that the practice of coloring eggs goes way, way back in history. Samuel told me that one time. Speaking of Samuel: Is something wrong with him? Lately he's been so harsh," Abigail said as she stood. "I'll let you know when I have all the items for the baskets. Oh, Ellie May, we'll count on your alto voice for our chorus," she said over her shoulder as she walked away.

"It's hard to believe that at one time Abigail was not liked at all. We did a good job when we matched her with William," Ellie May said proudly. "She has been remarkable since then. I think it's great she's giving the kids an egg hunt."

"The First Lady will be hosting an Easter egg hunt on the White House lawn on Easter Monday. They hunt for eggs and they roll them. I know they conduct other activities, too, like games and storytelling. Admittance is through a lottery that was held in February. I'd love to take Gretchen sometime. Rosebud, your Phillip, with all his connections, might know someone who knows someone to get me an invitation," Marty said happily.

Rosebud laughed. "I'll ask him tonight."

"Going out again? Wow, this is serious," Ellie May said. As she peered over the top of her wire-rimmed glasses, she said, "May I ask, what Phillip gave you for your birthday?"

"A cruise."

"Say what?" Ellie May responded.

"Keep this just among us. We'll be doing the Caribbean," Rosebud said, obviously delighted about the whole thing.

Just then they all spied the rabbit again. They smiled. Marty said quietly, "He sure is a persistent fellow, isn't he? Yes, I think he's really scouting out good places to hide Easter eggs."

"Ladies, since we were so successful in getting William and Abigail together, what do you say we try to match Julia with one of our eligible men?" Ellie May asked hopefully.

"Let's not spoil our perfect record when it comes to matchmaking," Marty suggested.

Ellie May was disappointed. That only left her detective work regarding the napkin thief to occupy her time. Well, she thought, if they aren't interested in matchmaking, she would put all her efforts into finding the missing napkins. She checked her watch. She better hurry to her apartment since there would be another segment of *True Detective* coming on shortly. Maybe the show might give her a new strategy to help her find her perp.

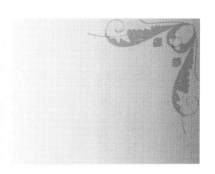

CHAPTER 10

William was pleased to discover the maintenance men already had moved the piano into Room C for the first meeting of the MGH Chorus. He was a bit nervous. While he had been a piano player for many years, traveling with a few bands, and lately, accompanying Abigail at her frequent appearances, he had never been responsible for a chorus. As soon as Abigail entered the room, his nerves were calmed. She had a powerful effect on him.

"Good morning, Abigail. Ready for our big day?" William asked as he held a chair for her.

"I don't know why we didn't think of this before, William. I believe we're going to enjoy this experience."

Their conversation was interrupted when a woman in a wheelchair appeared in the doorway.. "I guess I'm at the right place," she said shyly.

"If you want to be part of the chorus, yes, this is the place," William said as he approached her. "I'm William Williams and this is Abigail Becker."

"I'm Catherine Blessing. I just moved here about five weeks ago," she said softly as she guided her chair beside Abigail.

"Ho, ho, I'm here," Nigel said as he bounced into the room. "Catherine, hello again."

Catherine looked puzzled.

"I met you in the Exchange Room one day. Remember. I immediately claimed your donation for myself. I really like the blender you contributed," Nigel said as he winked at her.

A flustered Catherine replied, "Oh, I remember now. Is the blender working properly?"

"Just fine. By the way, William, I'm here to lend my bass voice to your chorus," Nigel gushed. "I hope we'll have more interested parties than just the few of us."

While Nigel was probably his best friend here at M, William hadn't been aware that in addition to his ballroom dancing, Nigel also liked to sing. "Thank you, Nigel."

Before too long, the crowd had swelled to twenty people. William was pleased. "First, let me welcome all of you. Abigail and I are delighted that you want to be part of our chorus. It is my hope that, from time to time, we'll be able to perform at various functions that are held here. To relieve your anxieties, we'll practice a few scales first and then just sing a few songs to warm up the vocal chords. I also want to hear each one of you separately." William saw that Catherine immediately put her hand over her mouth. "Nothing to worry about. It will give me an idea of where you will fit into the group. We intend to be very casual. We want you to have fun."

At first William could barely hear the chorus members' voices go up and down the scales. However, after the third time, the singers became more confident and their voices began to resonate throughout the room.

When evaluating members' voices, William was overjoyed to discover several of them had amazing ability. Ellie May and Catherine were outstanding. He was surprised to find that Nigel was as good as he had claimed to be.

"While we'll be expected to sing hymns from time to time, I want to include all types of music—hits from Broadway shows, some pop music, and, of course, to keep me happy, even some country-western." William said. "Please don't hesitate to suggest songs that you would like us to try. This is your chorus."

"Maybe we could even put a little show together to entertain at the ladies' tea thing, whatever it's called, or maybe even at the *Harvest Moon*—whatever it's called," Nigel said enthusiastically. "We have plenty of time to rehearse."

"Good idea, Nigel. Ladies and gentlemen, before you leave today, I would like you to take one of these index cards and jot down the titles of songs you would like us to try. It'll be a fun time, and we'll readily discover the tunes we can handle the best."

Ellie May tapped Catherine on the shoulder. "Catherine, I'm so glad to meet you. If you have any questions about the activities we have here, just give me a ring. Would you have time to have lunch with me today—my treat?"

"That's nice of you, but I have a doctor's appointment at noon. Perhaps next time," Catherine replied courteously as she wheeled herself out of the room.

As Ellie May headed to her apartment, she spotted one of the new servers pushing a tall cart of soiled laundry out of the dining room. She decided to follow her. Sure enough, the girl removed a key from her pocket and pushed the cart into the service elevator. She then leaned on the hold button and went back into the dining room. Ellie May knew this was her lucky day. She made her move and scurried into the elevator and stooped down behind the cart. As the young woman pushed the second cart into the service elevator, Ellie May felt like a true detective. Now she needed to get off without being seen. When the girl pushed the one cart off the elevator, Ellie May made her move. Clutching her shoes that she had removed, she kept her head below the cart and backed herself up against the wall. When the server had the second cart inside the laundry room, the young woman let out a sigh and slammed the door shut behind her.

While Ellie May was proud of what she had just done, she really didn't know what her next move should be. She had wanted to get into this room for a long time. Where would a seasoned detective begin? The cart. She needed to examine the cart. She began by counting the white napkins. By the time she was finished, she had no idea what that number would really tell her since she didn't know how many places had been set last night. However, she was excited when she realized that there was an odd number of napkins in the cart. All tables in the dining room were always set for an even number of guests.

Now she had proof that, once again, someone had taken some napkins, she was pleased with her cleverness. As she shook the last napkin on her pile, something plopped onto her foot. Immediately, she realized it was an ID tag for a dining room server. She immediately connected it to the girl who had slammed the door shut. Lucinda was her name.

Proud of her findings, Ellie May decided she should meet with Rebecca to tell her what she had discovered. Reaching for the door handle, she discovered it was locked. Knowing she didn't have her cell phone with her, she looked around the room for a house phone. There was none. She could hear the eerie sounds of some motors running steadily, echoing in her ears. Ellie May didn't panic until the lights went off.

CHAPTER 11

Stretch was enjoying his new position as Rebecca's assistant. He loved working days instead of the hours he used to put in when he was the baker and the manager of *The Night Owl*. He was learning a great deal and having such a good time that he felt he should pay MGH for allowing him to work. While it wasn't as exciting as when he was racing horses at the track and getting his picture taken in the Winner's Circle, he no longer had to worry about putting on weight and having to sit in the sweat box to get down to his jockey weight. While he missed the thrill of crossing the finish line first with his horse, he wouldn't miss some of the seedier things that happened at the track.

He wanted things to be perfect for dinner tonight in the dining room. It would be his first time to take care of everything since Rebecca wouldn't be in for a few days in order to have some kind of medical procedure. As he turned around to go back into the kitchen, he spied one of his servers huddled in the corner, crying. This shook him up. He knew how to calm nervous horses —putting a goat or a mirror in their stall so they would feel they had a stable mate—but how to deal with women was something new for him.

With tears streaming down her face, she looked up and said, "I've lost my ID tag and Wilma told me I'll be charged twenty-five dollars for a replacement."

Stretch said, "I remember seeing your ID tag on you as you left the dining room to take the linen cart down to the laundry room. When did you first notice it was gone?"

"Wilma noticed it when I went into the kitchen after I came up from downstairs," the sobbing girl related.

"Well, then, let's start there. Come with me." Stretch headed for the elevator. When they got off, Stretch immediately realized the door to the laundry room was closed tightly.

"Did anyone caution you not to completely close that door?" Stretch asked as gently as he could.

"No. Why not?" Lucinda asked.

"We keep it ajar since it automatically locks when it closes. Rather than giving out so many keys to the staff, it just seemed easier," Stretch explained. "But perhaps we need to revisit our idea. Preston could probably fix the problem for us."

As he inserted his key into the lock, he thought he heard a voice. He looked around. "Did you say something, Lucinda?"

"I thought I heard *help.*" Lucinda began looking around, all the while staying very close to Stretch.

Stretch, taking no chances, opened the door slowly as Lucinda hid behind him.

"Thank you, God," Ellie May said as soon as she saw Stretch.

Stretch instinctively knew he had to handle this situation very carefully. After all, Miss Ellie May was a paying resident. He couldn't imagine why she would be in the laundry room, but he thought it best if he found out without Lucinda being present. Maybe, just maybe, sitting in a sweat box really was easier.

"Lucinda lost her ID and…"

"Here it is," Ellie May said as she held it up. "I found it in the dirty laundry."

"Oh, thank you," Lucinda gushed as she grabbed it out of Ellie May's hands.

"Lucinda, you better go back upstairs and help with the place settings for tonight," Stretch recommended.

As soon as he heard the elevator door close, Stretch said, "Miss Ellie May," as he tried to stop smiling, "how did you get in here?"

Ellie May was embarrassed. "Stretch, I know this will sound crazy, but I was trying to find out who was stealing the napkins from the dining room. When I saw Lucinda getting on the elevator to take the laundry downstairs, I snuck in behind her and went along. I thought I might be able to find some clue—you know—evidence regarding the missing napkins. When the girl left the room, she pushed the door shut…and here I am."

At first, Stretch remained quiet. Then, he began to laugh. Suddenly, Ellie May, relieved by his reaction, joined in the laughter.

When they quieted down, Ellie May said, "Stretch, can we keep this between us?"

"Miss Ellie May you're a delight. I had no idea you could be such a fractious little filly," Stretch teased.

"Is that good or bad? I don't know anything about horses. I've never been to a race track. I did, however, see the Kentucky Derby on TV last year," Ellie May explained.

"When preparing two-year-old colts for racing, we practice putting them into the gate. This helps them get used to the sights and sounds that can be frightening the first time they experience them. Well, anyway, the little colts have minds of their own. Usually, instead of paying attention to the gate, they want to look at one another and just play. But once they discover what racing is all about, its all they want to do and they can become difficult to rein in. I guess you can tell I still miss racing. I'm thinking about purchasing a horse and stabling it at Rainbow Track," Stretch rambled. "But it all depends on what kind of deal I can arrange."

"That sounds exciting," Ellie May said. "Will you be the jockey?"

"No, I'm not jockey material any more. But, if I do get a race horse, I'll let you know when he runs and perhaps you can get to the track to watch. Now—getting back to Lucinda—since she got her ID back, she's a happy camper, who'll probably forget all about this before the day is over," Stretch said, hoping to make Ellie May feel better.

As Ellie May headed back to her apartment, she decided not to eat in the dining room tonight. Perhaps, if she waited a few days before going back there, Lucinda might not even remember her face. She wondered if the great Sherlock Holmes had ever done anything as dumb as she had. Well, that's probably the price I must pay as I develop my investigative skills. She loved thinking about herself as a fractious little filly. That's so much better than being a dumb cop.

CHAPTER 12

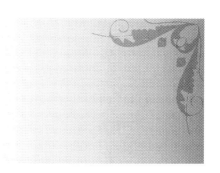

Samuel was shopping online. He needed to get a few things he had been unable to find locally. It irritated him to do this. But the stores within driving distance from MGH didn't carry the type of merchandise he wanted. Even though people seemed much more willing to accept those who classified themselves as LGTBQ, they had closed minds when it came to those who had needs outside the box.

Oscar, his beloved Siamese, was curled up at his feet. Oh, how he wished humans would be more like cats—they do whatever they want and they care less who approves of their behavior. Most of the time, Oscar ignored his owner. But, even a cat had special needs once in a while and that's when he allowed Samuel to pet him. Mainly, though, Samuel and Oscar got along because they tolerated one another.

"Well, Oscar, I didn't find anything today. I guess I'll take a break and go to the *Sassy Cat* for lunch." He was still angry since the residents had overwhelmingly voted to have cameras installed at the garage entrance—stupid cows. "I can't imagine why they allowed this to happen, Oscar," Samuel complained as he stood and closed the lid on his laptop. "Have a good nap. I'll be back before too long."

When he got to *The Square,* he spied a stack of the latest issue of *The Morning Glory Newsletter* on the front desk. He took a copy and found a comfortable seat on his favorite sofa and sat down to peruse the latest news. He skipped over the article about the cameras—he just didn't want to read anything about such an invasion of privacy. Just as he was examining a one-page advertisement for the upcoming *Harvest Moon Bazaar,* he heard a feminine voice call out his name.

"Oh, Dr. Long," Julia said sweetly, "didn't I see you in the audience the other day at the lecture given by Dr. Elmer Kleckner at Wood University?"

"Yes, I was there," Samuel replied in a disinterested voice.

"If you don't mind, Dr. Long, I would love to hear your evaluation of Dr. Kleckner's presentation. There just aren't many people, who live at this place, who have the ability to participate in an energized debate or diatribe about anything but a sporting event."

Suddenly, Samuel was interested. "My dear, you're the only resident who has ever acknowledged my title. I thank you for that."

Julia replied, "You deserve to receive respect, Doctor. Dr. Kleckner proposed some interesting challenges, regarding some of our long-held beliefs about the effectiveness of some of our past presidents. I found his talk fascinating. I'm thrilled to have the opportunity to talk with someone like you—you hold a doctorate in history and you probably could have given an even better speech than Dr. Kleckner," Julia gushed as she smiled at him.

Samuel didn't fail to notice when Julia moved a tad closer to him. She was not only an intelligent woman, she was also quite charming. She was the first woman he had ever met who caught his attention. Now, he must find out more about this intriguing female.

"Thank you for that compliment. You're a breath of fresh air. All I heard at breakfast this morning was talk about Easter bunnies and colored eggs. A man can only take so much of that kind of talk before he goes crazy. Julia, would you by chance like to join me for lunch? It would give me the time to explain my thoughts on the famous Dr. Kleckner."

"Dr. Long, I …"

"My dear—it's Samuel. I have a feeling we'll become friends very quickly. Please join me for lunch so we can talk about Dr. Kleckner and his theories," Samuel said as he stood and put his arm out. She smiled and they walked down Violet Lane to *The Sassy Cat*. This woman had caught his attention. She had obviously recognized his brilliance, while others at MGH were too uneducated to appreciate him. Most of the residents were as dumb as dirt. For a long time, Samuel had longed for someone to carry on an intellectual give- and-take. While Julia was his inferior, she wisely recognized quality when she saw it. Perhaps he could be her guide—a beacon to bring her out of the dark, dismal morass of ignorance.

Rosebud was seated at one of the tables with Marty and Frank and was the first to spot Julia and Samuel enter the deli. She was so surprised that she dropped her fork and sat with her mouth open for a few seconds. "And they say miracles don't happen."

As they covertly watched the couple make themselves comfortable in a booth, Rosebud said, "Gee, I wish I could hear what they're talking about. Julia is a grump and Samuel hates women—at least I thought he did. Look, they're both smiling!"

"I really haven't gotten to know Julia. She's just not interested in any of the activities that I've suggested," Marty remarked.

"Marty," Frank said, "perhaps Samuel can offer her the kind of activities that you cannot."

Rosebud immediately sat up straight. "Frank, I'm surprised at you. Are you suggesting…"

"Come on now, Rosebud," Frank replied as his face turned red.

"Rosebud, be careful," Marty cautioned. "Remember, you have Phillip and people could talk about that—you know what I mean."

"I guess you're right," Rosebud admitted. "Here comes Ellie May. Let's watch her as she passes by our newest couple."

Ellie May didn't disappoint. She stopped dead in her tracks as soon as she saw Julia and Samuel. They both looked up at her at the same time. A bit embarrassed, she hurriedly said, "Oh, hello, you two." She turned away and quickly took a seat beside Marty.

Quietly, Ellie May asked, "When did all of *that* happen?" she said as she pointed with her head at Samuel's table.

"Five minutes ago," Rosebud laughed. "How's the napkin detective doing?"

"I know, I know. It wasn't too smart getting locked in the laundry room. But I've another idea. Last night, there was a guest in the dining room in a wheel chair. And, as she went out the door, she suddenly stopped when she realized she still had her napkin in her lap. You know we have two regulars who use wheelchairs—Catherine and Rodney, the guy that just got back from rehab," Ellie May went on. "I consider them *persons of interest*. That would be a good way for someone to get out the door without anyone realizing that they still had a napkin."

"Ellie May, when are you going to stop this nonsense?" Rosebud asked. "My God, Rodney must be at least ninety! What on earth would he want with napkins?"

"I'll stop when I catch the thief and not before," Ellie May stated firmly. "Since you two won't help me, I have to do all the investigations by myself. Frank, do you think this is nonsense?"

"If you feel strongly about this, go ahead. If I can help in any way, let me know," Frank said kindly.

"See," Ellie May said haughtily, "someone believes in me. Okay, Frank, you keep an eye on Rodney tonight after dinner and I'll tail Catherine. We'll double-up on our perps."

"Not to change the subject, but Abigail wants us to help decorate the dining room tomorrow morning. Harvey has created some clever cardboard cut-outs, but they need extra hands to hang them up and to fill baskets and set up tables," Marty mentioned. "Ellie May, do you think you could stay out of trouble for a few hours so you can help us get ready for the Easter egg event?"

"Oh, I'm expected to help you, but you can't help me—I see," Ellie May said forlornly.

"Ellie May, you know I'll help you. When you want me to do anything, just tell me," Marty said.

"That goes for me, too," Rosebud added.

"Okay. I'll try to stay out of trouble, but I can't promise I will," Ellie May squeaked as she winked at Frank.

CHAPTER 13

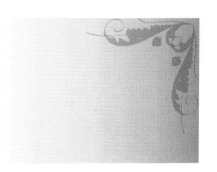

The elementary orchestra had finished their presentation for the residents of MGH and were packing up their instruments. While one half of the dining room had been closed off, and the children had no idea what was behind the folding doors, they were eager to get outside for the egg hunt. As Miss Abigail walked across the stage and picked up the microphone, they quieted down immediately.

"Since you have treated us to such a splendid concert, we have a few surprises for you. Mr. Harvey, will you please open the folding doors?"

As the other half of the dining room became visible, the children were delighted to see large cardboard bunnies, holding bunches of brightly colored balloons, standing around the room. The luncheon tables were decorated with tiny paper rabbits and miniature bags of jelly beans. Servers were bringing out trays of little sandwiches and fruit cups.

"There will be more surprises for you if you eat your lunch including the fruit," she directed as she walked back and forth. "You'll need energy to participate in the egg hunt."

"Miss Abigail, may we eat the jellybeans?" one little boy asked.

"After you eat your lunch, you may eat a few," Abigail replied.

A little later, William picked up the microphone. "Now that you're finished with your lunch, it's time to welcome a very special visitor. Miss Rosebud, will you please open the door for our guest?"

When the children spotted Nigel, dressed in a fuzzy, white bunny suit, hopping through the door pushing a wheelbarrow filled with stuffed bunnies, they squealed with delight. Nigel hopped around the room as his long pink ears flopped around his head.

"The Easter Bunny has a rabbit for everyone. Now wait," William cautioned, "you must first complete a dance with Mr. Bunny. Miss Abigail will help you form a line behind him. That's it...now put your hands on the waist of the person standing in front of you. I'll sing the song and you follow my directions. Mr. Frank and Miss Marty will demonstrate first—watch them carefully."

Frank and Marty had moved to the front of the stage and waited for their cue.

William played a few notes, and then he began singing, "Put your right foot in, put your left foot out, join in the fun, and shake it all about, do bunny hop, hop, hop, hop."

As Frank and Marty hopped across the stage, a chorus of noisy laughter greeted them. The children could hardly contain themselves as they watched the demonstration. When Frank and Marty stopped hopping, Nigel began hopping up and down as his large pink ears wobbled around his head. "Children, the Easter Bunny is ready to dance, are you?" William asked. Hearing a resounding *yes* from the children, he said, "Okay, here we go."

Nigel was a big hit with the children. He was having just as much fun as they were. When William stopped playing, he said, "Now, children, you may chose a bunny from the wheelbarrow. When you all have one, we'll go outside for the egg hunt."

It was a perfect day for an egg hunt. The sun was shining and a slight breeze made it even more delightful. Abigail led the way to the lawn with the children tagging along behind her. After she gave each child a paper bag, she said, "Drop your rabbit in the bag so you don't lose it. The Easter Bunny has hidden a lot of eggs all over the area surrounded with pink ribbons. Put the eggs you find in your bag. When the bunny blows his whistle, you may begin. When the hunt is over, please return here to get an Easter basket filled with candies to take home,"

By now the children were extremely excited. "Miss Abigail," Rusty said as he tugged on her skirt, "This is the best party of my whole life."

Abigail reached down and gave the child a hug. Being the patron of the elementary school orchestra was the best thing that she had ever done. While her marriage had been a disappointment—and she had been unhappy for years— the children renewed her faith in God and made her whole again. She smiled as she thought about the good things that her husband's money had done. A cheater and a verbal abuser, her husband redeemed himself by leaving her a small fortune. Now, of course, she also had William. She liked to think of William and the children as her family. Who said there were no second chances?

Soon the lawn was filled with children laughing and shouting as they discovered the eggs and hurriedly put them in their bags. Rosebud was sitting in the gazebo as Rusty came running in. She casually pointed to an egg that the Easter Bunny had placed between the slats of the bench. As Rusty put the egg in his bag, he blew Rosebud a kiss.

Before long, the children were lined up to get their Easter baskets. Abigail gathered them together and led them across the parking lot to the school bus that was waiting to take them home. Abigail gave each child a hug as they climbed up the steps, trying hard not to spill the contents of their baskets.

Just then a taxi pulled up to the entrance of MGH. Rosebud strained her neck to see who was arriving. She jumped with glee when she saw Gordon and Marie Turnbull, returning from a trip to Nassau. Gordon, a retired Bahamian lawyer, had traveled to his native island to take care of his father's estate. Rosebud had missed Marie since the two of them did quite a lot of shopping together. They both loved fashion and they never missed a fifty-percent-off sale.

Rosebud hurried across the lawn. "Marie...Gordon... welcome home!"

No one seemed to notice that in all the hubbub of the day's events, Samuel and Julia were nowhere in sight. As Nigel, still in his bunny suit, was hopping around *The Square*, having a bit of fun with some of the residents, he walked past the elevator to the garage. The doors opened and Julia and Samuel appeared, each carrying a small satchel. They seemed flustered. Nigel didn't fail to notice that the two of them exchanged knowing expressions.

"Did all go well for you, Easter Bunny?" Samuel said sarcastically.

Nigel, who had a funny remark to make most of the time, was silent.

"Just to let you know—my dear friend Julia and I didn't see any menacing strangers running around the garage. I guess the cameras scared them all away," Samuel quipped, as he winked at Julia.

Nigel stood still. Something was awry. Something didn't fit. He couldn't put his finger on it—but Samuel was now in his radar. While Ellie May was still chasing the napkin bandit, Nigel had a sense this could be a bigger, more salacious happening than missing linens. He wouldn't say anything to Ellie May because she might steal this mystery from him. Nigel made himself a promise: He would get the goods on Samuel and perhaps knock the professor off his educational highfalutin ladder. From the time he was a child, Nigel had had an uncanny ability to read people. Samuel could go ahead and make fun of him all he wanted— Nigel was going to win in the end.

CHAPTER 14

An intimate group of residents of Morning Glory Hill was assembling in Marty's apartment for a *Welcome Home* party for the Turnbulls. Gordon and Marie had returned home after spending three months in the Bahamas, Gordon's native country. Gordon's brother, Winston, had died as the result of an auto accident. He had appointed Gordon as the executor for handling his sizeable estate. Marty also was using this party to welcome Enid's daughter, Helena, who was visiting her mother for several weeks from Las Vegas. Marty not only invited her close friends, but she had made a special trip to Julia's to encourage her to attend. She didn't tell her that Enid was coming and bringing Helena along. Marty hoped that she hadn't made a mistake by inviting the sisters to the little celebration. But, then again, perhaps this was the ideal time for Julia to be civil, especially since her niece would also be coming.

William and Frank were setting up the bar while Nigel stood at the door, acting as host. He wasn't surprised that Sally was the first to arrive. Every time the doorbell rang, he opened the door with a flourish, hoping that it would be Helena. He had never before met anyone who actually lived and worked in his favorite town, Las Vegas. Getting a bit restless, he opened the door to peek down the lane—no one was coming. He decided to get a drink, and just as he took his first sip, the doorbell rang. Rushing to the door, he opened it quickly and stood back. There was Enid with an attractive lady by her side. "Welcome, Enid," he said. "I'm assuming that this pretty lady is your daughter."

"Helena, this is the dancer I was telling you about. Nigel, this is Helena and *yes*, she still works in Las Vegas," Enid teased as she laughed.

"May I get you ladies a drink? " Nigel offered as he pointed to the bar.

"How about some wine, Helena?" Enid asked.

With wine glasses in hand, Enid began escorting her daughter around the room. She was pleased that she didn't see Julia. But her pleasure didn't last long as Marty shortly welcomed Julia to the party. Enid was apprehensive regarding how Julia and Helena would greet one another. When Marty had first invited her to the party, Enid was going to decline because of a long-standing friction between Helena and her Aunt Julia. For some reason, those two had had a falling out some time ago and had, ever since, kept their distance from one another. Enid had tried to quiz Helena about the animosity, but Helena always dismissed the question. However, the room came alive as soon as the handsome Bahamian and his wife arrived. Julia was obviously impressed with Gordon and Marie. Marty didn't fail to notice that Julia kept turning her back to Helena—off to a troublesome start.

Harvey shook Gordon's hand and said, "Gordon, old chap, we missed you. Glad you're back. Harry and I absolutely love the Bahamas. *Treasure Cay* is breathtaking—over three miles of pristine beaches—and those mansions—wow, I would simply die to get inside one of them."

"When we were there," Harry whispered, "Harvey really was hoping to find some pirates, still lurking around the cay, looking for Spanish wrecks. He does have an over-active mind," Harry said playfully. "He would have passed out if he had actually come across Blackbeard."

"My country is rich in history—some of which we are proud. Did you know that during World War II, the Allies centered their flight training and antisubmarine operations for the Caribbean in the Bahamas?"

"No, I didn't realize that. When most Americans think of the Bahamas, they imagine swashbuckling pirates and their quest for ships filled with gold. I believe our impression of the Bahamas was shaped by the film industry," William stated.

"One of the Bond films, I think the fourth one, was partially filmed in Nassau. That was around 1965 or so," Gordon added. "I have to admit, though, while we have homes that can sell for as much of fifty million, the country is still dealing with issues involving education and health care."

"Sounds a bit like the USA," Nigel joked.

Enid steered Helena to where William and Abigail were standing. "Helena, this is our Abigail—she has a fantastic voice. We're in the chorus together," Enid said proudly.

"Your mother is very gracious, but do you know that she has a melodic alto voice? Well, she does. The chorus is going to sing at the Ladies' Tea to be held in May. I hope you're still here then," Abigail said as she shook hands with Helena.

"Mom used to sing in the church choir," Helena said as she put her arm around her mother's waist. "But I haven't heard her sing for a long time."

Nigel began to circulate and eventually got the chance to talk with Helena alone. He kept asking her questions, but she didn't seem to mind. She even laughed at some of his jokes. "Nigel, when you come to Vegas, make sure you contact me. I'll show you the town as you should see it," Helena said as she patted his arm.

In another part of Marty's living room, Julia was trying to impress Gordon. "I have some money I'd like to invest. How about the Bahamas? Can you recommend anything there for me?"

"I must caution you that properties in the Bahamas can range from fifty million down to several million. While there are some homes under a million, they are few and far between. If you're serious about investing there, I recommend you personally visit the islands and select an agent. If you decide to do that, I can offer you a few recommendations. You know, choosing a real-estate agent is a bit like choosing a doctor—you need someone that you can relate to—someone in whom you can place your trust."

"I appreciate your advice, Gordon," Julia said.

"However, you may want to consider purchasing a property, let's say, with a small group of people. That way the purchase price can be shared and each one would have their turn residing at the property. Unless you plan on making the home you purchase your permanent residence, you'll need an agency to rent the property on a weekly or monthly basis. You certainly wouldn't want the property not to be maintained while you're not there. Your agent would be responsible for the maintenance of the property and for keeping it secure. That way you would be earning money to put towards the upkeep and agent fees and such," Gordon said. "Your fees would be based on the amenities that your property offers. While you won't have renters all the time, you can earn a sizable sum with part-timers. In fact, that's what Marie and I are doing with the home we inherited from my father. We figure that that will give us enough time to decide where we really want to live permanently."

"Gordon, what about…"

"Julia, for heaven's sake, let the man alone. This is a party," Enid whispered to her sister.

"Just because you don't know how to take care of *your* money, don't criticize me for being smarter than you."

Julia was loud enough for Helena to overhear the conversation. She walked over to Julia and said, "Aunt Julia, may I please see you in the den? This is important." She put her hand on her aunt's elbow and guided her out of the room.

"Aunt Julia, I'm going to tell you this one time. No… don't back away, or if you do, I'll hold this conversation in the living room. Now, if I ever hear that you have insulted or berated my mother again, I will tell all that I know about you to those people out there."

"Oh, is that supposed to scare me?" Julia said haughtily. "You sound high and mighty for someone who works in the gambling industry."

"I'm certain no one knows about the patent leather *Mary Jane* shoes, now, do they?" Helena snarled knowingly as she stared pointedly at her aunt.

Julia turned white. "I don't know what you mean."

"Okay, let's go out there to finish this dialog."

Julia looked away. "I don't know what..."

"Yes, you do. I don't want to contact Roger."

"I forbid you to contact my son," Julia said harshly.

"You cannot forbid me to do anything. Now, do I have your promise that you will **never, never** insult my mom again?" Helena said forcefully.

Julia pursed her lips. She blinked her eyes several times. Finally, she asked, "Did your grandmother tell you this?"

"Doesn't matter how I found out—I know. For the last time, shall I go out there and share what I know with those people, or do I have your promise to start respecting my mother?"

Reluctantly, Julia said, "I promise."

CHAPTER 15

Jake Lombardo, the new manager of *The Night Owl*, was settling into his routine. He had just removed a tray of cookies from the oven when he heard some customers enter the shop. Since this was only his second night taking care of the shop, he was apprehensive about whether or not he would be able to fill the shoes of the retired jockey whose place he took. He had met Stretch and liked the man, but was a bit jealous that Stretch was so well liked by the staff. When he thought about the jockey's boots, he laughed. Here Jake was, a stocky six foot two guy, who looked like anything but a jockey—Jake's feet would never fit into Stretch's small boots.

Pushing the swinging door open, Jake was relieved when he spotted William and Nigel, the only two customers he had had last night. "Hi, guys. Nice seeing you again," Jake said.

"It sure smells good in here, Jake. What's baking?" Nigel asked as he rubbed his belly.

"Old-fashioned snickerdoodles," Jake replied. "Want to try some?"

"Sure, why not?" Nigel murmured.

"You, too?" Jake said as he looked at William.

"You bet. But tonight I think I would like some tea," William said almost in a whisper.

"I told you before," Nigel muttered, "tea is **not** a man's drink."

"Don't pay him any attention, Jake. Nigel has some far-out ideas," William joshed.

Just then, Enid entered the little shop. "Got room for me?" she asked timidly.

Nigel jumped up and got a chair for Enid. "Any time, my dear. I'm going to miss your daughter. She's a charmer. Why, do you know she said that if I visit Vegas, I could stay at her place? Isn't that nice, William?" Nigel quipped. "But I wouldn't want to be a bother."

"Oh, Nigel. Helena has a little guest cottage alongside her home. She would love to have you stay there. You could take a bus or a cab to get to any of the casinos," Enid explained.

"If Nigel goes to Vegas, he may never come back," William teased. "Now, wait a minute, that's not a bad idea. I'm sure I could get a lot of people to chip in to buy him a one-way ticket," William said as he laughed.

"Oh, you'd miss me," Nigel said assuredly.

"By the way, Nigel, you made an excellent bunny for the children at the egg hunt. You made them so happy. They loved dancing with you, or I guess I should say *hopping* with you. You certainly have a way with children," Enid said sweetly.

"It's my charm," Nigel said as he puffed out his chest.

"Enid, I saw you and Harvey working in the Tech Room the other day. Are you taking computer lessons?" William asked.

"Yes, but he's also helping me with my idea for the *Harvest Moon Bazaar*. I can type, but I never had worked on a computer before. Harvey helped me expand my idea which requires me to do some writing. And, Harry's also helping me. But I'm keeping my idea a secret," Enid crowed, obviously pleased with the whole idea. "Harvey thinks what I will be doing could possibly win first place."

"Harvey's a genius with decorating and design and Harry's a prize-winning photographer. You guys will be hard to beat," Nigel pouted. "I don't know what I can make or do that would be worth a prize."

"I'm surprised at you, Nigel. All you have to do is build a small dance floor and offer to teach some dance steps. The ladies will go wild," Enid offered. excitedly.

"Do you really think that would work?"

"My, yes. Maybe you and Rosebud could work as a team. She could teach the gentlemen and you could charm the ladies off their feet," Enid suggested.

"What about you, William?" Nigel pressed. "You sure as hell can't teach anyone to play the piano in a few minutes, now, can you?"

"I do have an idea, but I am **not** going to tell you. You'll blab to everyone," William responded.

"Sounds like an argument might be going on," Frank said cautiously as he entered the shop.

"Hi, Frank. We haven't seen you lately. Everything okay?" Nigel asked.

"I'm okay. Remarkably, I've been sleeping much better lately. Well, that is, before tonight. I was hoping I'd find someone here," Frank said as he joined the group. He didn't want to mention that he had been wrestling with a decision that could impact his future. This was not the time or place to talk about his concerns. Perhaps he could arrange to speak with William in private.

"We were just talking about what we're going to do for the *Harvest Moon Bazaar*. Are you going to be making something in the wood shop? I saw the dollhouse you made for Marty's great-granddaughter. If that wasn't a prize-winner, I don't know what is," William pointed out. "However, Enid and Nigel plan on giving you a run for your money."

"Nigel, you were the best bunny I have ever seen hopping," Frank interjected. "The kids loved you."

"Well, I must confess, I went to *Bunny School* to learn how to hop properly," Nigel said convincingly.

"Maybe you guys talked about this already, but what are your opinions on having cameras at our garage entrance?" Frank asked. "I understand that Samuel is not too happy with them."

"Well, maybe the old boy, has something to hide. I'm a firm believer that one can find out a lot by paying attention to who complains the most about something," Nigel said as he shook his head up and down.

"Meaning what?" William asked.

"My instincts have always been good. I'm not sure, yet, but I know he's up to something. He has the look," Nigel insisted.

"The look?"

"Yeah, you know—the kind of look the fox has on his face when he comes out of the hen house," Nigel replied.

"Nigel, you talk in circles. What has Samuel got to do with a fox and a hen house?" William asked impatiently.

"Think about it for a minute. I guess you never lived on a farm," Nigel said contritely.

"Nigel, Nigel, Nigel," William said. 'I'm just about ready to buy you a ticket to Vegas myself."

"You may doubt me now, but I'm willing to bet you a ticket to Vegas that Samuel is hiding a big secret. Do you have enough courage to take me up on this bet—or are you a chicken?" Nigel spouted.

"You got it. It's a bet."

CHAPTER 16

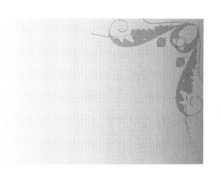

Stretch could hardly contain himself. Now he could take one item off his bucket list. He had claimed a race horse at the track last night. He and his trainer, Butch Orr, had put in a claim for a horse that was in the last race at Rainbow Race Track and Casino. Stretch had been a nervous wreck as the two of them watched the horse in the paddock as her trainer was preparing her to run in a $10,000 claiming race. They were not permitted to go inside the area to examine the horse, All they could do was judge her on how she conducted herself.

Butch said, "She looks good. Her walk is steady and she seems to be alert, but calm. I'll go in the office and put in our claim. You must wait here," he said as he left the trembling retired jockey leaning heavily on the fence.

"Hey there, Stretch," a gruff voice hollered. "Are you back riding?"

"Nah. My riding days are over. Butch and I just put in a claim for number seven, LUCKY LADY," Stretch replied as he tried to calm down.

"Well," the stranger said, "I wish you luck. You were one hellava jockey!"

When the post parade began, Stretch and Butch walked down to the Winner's Circle to watch the race. "I hope she comes out of the race sound," Butch said as he watched the horse intently.

Stretch thought about the amount of money that the horse was costing. He knew that if LUCKY LADY would break down during the race, she might have to be euthanized—he would be buying a dead horse with his ten grand. Trying not to think of anything negative, Stretch lifted his binoculars and focused only on the beautiful gray filly.

"She's a beauty," Stretch said. Quietly, Stretch said a little prayer, just as he used to do every time that he heard the words *riders up*. He was experiencing the same feelings— the sensation that he loved when he had guided his horse into the Winner's Circle years ago. Now, with illness and bones that no longer responded to his needs, Stretch could only rely on old memories. The noise of the starter button at the starting gate, even though Stretch had heard that ring hundreds of times, sent shivers up his spine. Jeff Turner, the current outstanding jockey at the track, was on LUCKY LADY'S back. He skillfully guided her through the pack of twelve horses and was laying third until the stretch run. Jeff tapped the filly lightly with his whip, asking for a bit more. The horse lifted her head a bit, perked her ears, and left all the other horses behind her. Butch was right—she was a closer.

Stretch breathed a sigh of relief. The only disadvantage of her winning was that the horse would have to be moved up in class the next time she ran unless she was idled for a month. But making the decision of when and where to run her next would be a joint effort between Butch and him. While Stretch knew a great deal about horses, he would be paying Butch a monthly fee to take care of LUCKY LADY. Every trainer had their own style and Stretch had long admired how Butch seemed to be able to get the best out of his horses with the least amount of problems. While horse racing was not an exact science, Stretch knew four factors must come together to produce a winner: A good jockey on the horse contributed twenty-five percent. Having a good trainer also provided twenty-five percent. A good horse would add forty percent. But the last ten percent was just plain luck. Stretch thought to himself that LUCKY LADY had lived up to her name.

"Well, Stretch, she's coming back just fine. If no one else has put in a claim for her, she'll be yours."

Stretch simply had forgotten that part. Now, what would he do if someone else got the horse he wanted so desperately? He knew that if that happened, there would be a draw to determine who got the horse.

Butch leaned over and whispered into Stretch's ear, "Nah, there were no other claims. Now, get ready to meet your first horse."

After the pictures had been taken with the horse and her previous owners, Stretch stepped inside the Winner's Circle and took the reins of his new possession. Stretch felt as if he had been walking on air as he led the horse to her new barn. It was very early in the morning before they had LUCKY LADY properly prepared to stay in her new stall. Butch had taken an extreme amount of time checking her out and hot-walking her. Finally, he had said, "She's fine. Now you go home. You and I will talk tomorrow about some ideas I have for her training and where I want to race her next."

The next morning, as soon as Rebecca arrived at Morning Glory Hill, Stretch cornered her. "Rebecca, I need to talk with you. Have a few minutes?"

"Sure. You look flushed. Are you okay?" she asked.

Stretch couldn't get his story out fast enough. Rebecca listened intently. "Does this mean we're going to lose you?" she asked hesitantly.

"Oh, no. I can't ride any more—at least not in races. I'll be able to help with her workouts and stuff, but that will be early in the morning. My trainer will take care of her. Oh, Rebecca, wait until you see her—a gorgeous four-year-old filly—full wide tail—sparkling dark eyes. She is sixteen hands and has good confirmation. Her mane is still light and she has a blaze on her nose."

"Maybe you should call her Morning Glory," Rebecca suggested.

"Oh, no. At the track, a horse who performs well in the morning, but fails to reproduce that in races is called a morning glory," Stretch emphasized. "She will remain LUCKY LADY."

"I'm getting to think you really like this horse, Stretch. When will we get an opportunity to see her?" Rebecca inquired.

"I think she might be ready in three weeks. We have to move her up in class, so we have a find a race that fits her," Stretch explained.

"Stretch, I think this is great. I don't know anything about racing, so you'll have to teach me," Rebecca reminded him.

"If I ever need time off, I'll make sure you know ahead of time," Stretch said, hoping she wouldn't object to what he had just said.

"We may have to rent a bus when she runs in order to take us all to the track. I'll have to get someone to take over the dining room on that night—I'm assuming she'll run at night?"

"For now, she will. If we ship to another track, that might change. Oh, Rebecca, I've never spent this much money at one time. People will think I'm crazy," Stretch said all the while smiling broadly. "I must tell Ellie May. Remember when I found her in the laundry room? We talked about horses."

"Well, when you see her, make sure you tell her that it seems that we no longer have a napkin thief. For the past four weeks, our napkin count has checked out," Rebecca said. "She was so dedicated to catching the thief that she may be devastated to learn the problem appears to be over."

CHAPTER 17

Marty and Frank were sitting in the gazebo enjoying the warm, late April evening. Frank kept looking over at Marty, not sure if he was brave enough to go through with his planned proposal. He kept feeling for the box that was buried in his jacket pocket, making sure it was still there. He had visited the jewelry store several times before he found a ring that he thought she would like. But then, he had finally come to the realization that the only thing he had to worry about was whether or not she would say *yes*—something only under her control. He had stood before his dresser mirror a dozen times, practicing his speech. He tried emphasizing their compatibility, but that seemed too mechanical. But, after all, they did get along and had very similar beliefs. He wondered what a woman would really want to hear during a proposal—probably something romantic—a subject that still made him nervous.

For a long time, Frank had wanted to broach the topic of marriage to Marty—but he had been fearful. He couldn't remember when a woman had been in his mind and his heart. His wife had died very young and he had had no desire to marry again—until he met Marty. One night in

The Night Owl, William talked about the arrangement that he and Abigail had. William had said that neither of them wanted to marry, so they pledged their love to one another and they had been happy ever since. William had gushed, "Friends with benefits, and I love it." Frank, however, hadn't been brought up that way. One of his daughters had such an arrangement, and while he disapproved of the situation, he had accepted it since he unconditionally loved his daughter.

Frank wanted to wake up in the morning with Marty beside him. He wanted to see her sitting across the breakfast table from him. Late in the night, he wanted to be able to reach across his bed and touch her. He longed for a traditional marriage. While he realized that the two of them needed to talk things over, and lots of decision would have to be made, he was willing to do all of that. Now, here they were, alone in the night. No one was around. A romantic setting just like in the movies.

Marty turned to him and said, "Frank, just this morning I thought about the necklace that had caused me so many problems," she said as she laughed a bit. "When I found it in my husband's old Dopp kit, I was shocked. I don't know where my head was when I wondered if he might had gotten it through an illegal transaction. Can you imagine that?"

"Well, you did say that he had had some strange friends. You also thought that the diamonds were real. It was only natural for you to make such an assumption," Frank said reassuringly.

"That's so like you, Frank. You can always make me see things in a different light. And, your idea of putting that damned thing in the fireman's boot, when they were collecting for charity, was simply the best thing that could have happened to that necklace. While the stones were not real, it still brought in several thousand dollars when it was auctioned off. You're a wise man, Frank," Marty said tenderly as she patted his hand.

Frank sat up straight. There would probably never be a more appropriate time to propose than right now. "Marty," he said softly as he turned to face her. "You must know by now how I feel about you."

Marty's eyes opened wide. Putting her hand over her mouth, she appeared to be dazed.

Frank reached into his pocket. He held the little velvet box in his hand and slowly opened it. "Marty, sweetheart—I never called you that before—will you marry me?"

Marty's silence frightened Frank. He felt as if his heart had stopped beating. Perhaps it would be better if he would die, right here on the spot, rather than hear a rejection.

"Frank, my dear, sweet Frank, are you sure?" Marty whispered.

"From the moment I met you, I knew you were the one. I guess that sounds corny. I'm not used to saying sweet little nothings, Marty. I don't know how to do that. But I can promise that I will always love you. What do you say, Marty?" Frank asked hopefully.

"Frank, oh, Frank…yes…yes."

Frank put his arms around her. She snuggled close and Frank was overjoyed. He had waited for this for a long, long time.

He took the ring out of the box as Marty lifted her hand towards him. Slowly, with trembling hands, he slipped it on her finger.

"Frank, this is beautiful, absolutely beautiful," she said. "It's perfect."

"I know we have lots to talk about and plans to make—like where we'll live—when will we tell our kids—and when we'll tie the knot," Frank said nervously. "I want you to know, Marty that I'm well-off financially, so we won't have to worry if one of us becomes ill and needs care. I know this isn't something that most couples who just get engaged talk about, but then most people who get engaged are not as old as we are," Frank chided.

"I have one favor to ask, Frank. Please tell your girls immediately. I'll break the news to my Daniel. I don't want our children to hear about this second-hand," Marty said. "Meanwhile, we'll have to take our time in working out all the details. Maybe a small intimate wedding will be best. I think we'll be happier if we stay right here—and--and, Frank, am I making any sense?"

"Well, I'm happy that you said *yes* and that's all the sense I need. May I kiss you, Marty?"

She lifted her head and their lips met. The kiss was warm and tender, not at all like the kiss she had seen on TV last night when she thought the guy was going to swallow the girl's tongue. "Frank, from now on, you don't have to get my permission to kiss me. Like the NIKE slogan--Just do it!"

CHAPTER 18

"But, Mom, all I want is for you to be happy and well-taken-care-of. I think Frank's a great guy. You certainly don't need my approval to marry the man," Daniel said.

"I was worried. I need your approval. I do want to get some of my financial things worked out with you. So if you..."

"Wow, Mom, we've been through this before. I **do not** need any financial help. If you want you could leave something for Gretchen. I've already established a trust fund for her for college, but a few extra bucks won't hurt," Daniel said patiently. "Too bad you don't have a valuable diamond necklace to give her," Daniel teased.

"Oh, you rascal. I feel another sermon coming on. I know...I know. I should have told you about that damned thing as soon as I found it, but honey—"

"It's okay, Mom. I was just pulling your chain a bit. If you want me to set something up with a lawyer, I'll do that. But, Mom, you've got to face it. Frank's the one who has lots to protect. He's a wealthy man. I know that he'll take good care of you. Your pensions will continue to come in, but you two must think about the ramifications that long-term care could have on your finances," Daniel cautioned.

"I hate to think about that. I love Frank. I have for quite some time. My monthly pensions will see me through if I lose him. Besides, I'm as healthy as a horse. I really won't need any of his money. After all, he has four daughters and several grandchildren to think about," Marty reminded Daniel.

"If Frank sets up a meeting with his attorney for the two of you, and you want me to go along, I will," Daniel said as he headed for the front door. "But knowing Frank, I don't think you'll have anything to worry about. He surely knows that you're not a gold digger," Daniel said as he laughed.

"You know what Frank said on the phone last night...you won't believe this. When he said he thought I was beautiful, then, I said that's good because I've always wanted to be a trophy wife," Marty said playfully.

"Mom—you'll never change. I'm afraid Frank won't know what hit him until it's too late. I better warn him," Daniel said as he kissed his mom on the cheek. "Now, I've got to run. I need to shop for a wedding gift for a couple who already has everything."

After Daniel was gone, Marty picked up her *To Do List*. She wanted to talk with Marie, the fashion expert of MGH, about what she should wear for the wedding. But then, it might be too early to make that kind of decision. She jumped when the doorbell rang. Thinking that it might be Daniel returning for some reason, she called out, "Come in."

The door opened and there stood Frank's four daughters. They suddenly burst into the room and, in unison, they said, "We're getting a new Mommie!"

"Girls, what a nice surprise," Marty said as Cora, June, Lucy and Delores each hugged her.

"Marty, it's been a long time since anyone has called us *girls*—that is except for Dad. My goodness, we're all fifty plus years," Cora said. "Oh, let me see the ring."

"Yes, yes, I want to see it, too," June said excitedly.

As Frank's daughters looked over the ring their dad had put on Marty's finger, they couldn't stop complimenting the good taste their dad had for not only jewelry, but for choosing Marty as his wife.

Marty could not have been more pleased. "I still cannot believe it," she said. "You don't think we're moving too fast, do you?"

Lucy replied, "My goodness, we've been waiting umpteen years for a mother—that's a lot of years. Anyway, we welcome you to the family with open arms. If there's anything you would like us to do for the wedding, just let us know."

"I guess I am too old to be a flower girl," Lucy said sadly.

"You can say that again," June said.

When the doorbell rang again, Lucy jumped up and said, "I'll get it, Mom."

Marie, Rosebud and Ellie May were standing there with their arms full of bridal magazines. "Hi, is Marty here?"

"Oh, you mean Mom?" Cora teased.

As the ladies introduced themselves to one another, the excitement level grew exponentially. Marie placed the magazines on the dining room table and said, "How about we sit over here. I'm sure Marty has dozens of things she wants to talk about and these might help," she said as she pointed to the magazines. "But we can't begin to make suggestions about bridal attire until Marty lets us know where and when this fabulous wedding will be taking place."

"Should Frank be here?" Ellie May asked.

"Heavens, no." Cora said. "Dad gave us strict orders that anything Marty wants is okay with him."

"Wouldn't it be romantic if they eloped?" Ellie May asked.

"No. no," Lucy said firmly. "We sisters have waited over forty-six years for a mother and we won't be deprived of a wedding."

Marty laughed, "Ellie May, can't you just picture Frank putting a ladder up to my bedroom window, my climbing out on the sill, and getting down the ladder—all of this without breaking a leg? Besides, I live on the first floor."

"Well, maybe you could just step out the window," Ellie May giggled.

"Did you pick a date yet, Marty?" Marie asked.

"We looked over the calendar of events for MGH and we've it narrowed down to either the first or third week in September. I was thinking about October, but the *Harvest Moon Bazaar* is scheduled for that time. I'm kinda partial to the first Saturday in September. The weather is usually beautiful around that time," Marty said enthusiastically.

"And, where will the wedding be?" Marie asked.

"We want to be married here…in the dining area. I'm sure that Harvey would be able to create a remarkable setting. What do you think?" Marty asked her friends.

"We should be making a list of things you need to do so that nothing falls between the cracks," Rosebud recommended.

"Will you do that?" Marty asked Rosebud.

"Certainly. So far, you need to contact Barry to schedule all the areas you'll require, and you need to talk with Harvey regarding the ambiance that you would like to have," Rosebud said as she began taking notes.

"You should begin to look for your outfit. You shouldn't wait too long to do that since you might need alterations and such," Marie suggested.

Cora was waiting patiently to speak. She couldn't wait any longer. "Marty, did you give any thought to your wedding party? I mean, you know—who else will be in the wedding?"

"I want you, Rosebud and you, Ellie May to be my matrons of honor. And, I would be so happy if my new daughters would be my bridesmaids," Marty asked hopefully as she smiled at her entourage. "Marie, I would like you to serve as the wedding coordinator. Of course, my darling Gretchen will be the flower girl. Daniel has already agreed to give me away. In fact, he said that he would be most happy to turn me over to someone else," Marty said as she laughed.

Frank's daughters were all talking at the same time. They were overjoyed with the idea of being in the wedding. The women were flipping through the bridal magazines, and suggestions were being offered all around the table.

"Oh, you'll have to talk with Frank about who he wants in the wedding. After all, he's an important part of this whole thing," Ellie May reminded them. "Put that on the list, Rosebud."

"Okay," Rosebud replied. "One groom needed!"

CHAPTER 19

"Enid, I can't believe that you're lending your teapots to the *Tiptoe Thru the Tulips Tea*. Aren't you afraid that someone might break one of them?" Harvey asked as he pushed the cart load of teapots down Daffodil Lane.

"I'm not letting them use all my teapots—I'm holding four of them back. But I thought it would be an ideal time for Harry to take pictures of them for the book I'm creating for the *Harvest Moon Bazaar*," Enid said graciously.

"I bet you kept your *Brown Betty*," Harvey teased.

"Oh, that one is still sitting on the middle shelf of my china closet," Enid replied. "It will only leave my apartment when they carry me out of there—feet first. Marty told me that last year they had to run all over the place to gather enough teapots for the event. This is the least I can do to make it a bit easier this year. I thought that the ladies, who all will be dressed in their finery for the tea, will be delighted to have their pictures taken for the book. I think it will be so authentic to have photos like that—what do you think?"

"You're right on target with that idea—a great setting! Harry can't wait to start this project. He'll meet us in the dining room to take a few practice shots before the tea begins at two," Harvey said.

"I need to get these down to the kitchen early so they can wash them properly. After all, they've been stored in my china closet for several months now," Enid said. "But I better supervise the washing just in case. Or, do you think I'm a worry wart?"

"The teapots are your pride and joy, Enid. It's alright to want to take care of them. Harry feels the same way about every photo he takes—always worrying if his clients view the photos with the same eagle-eye as he does."

As they approached the entrance to the dining room, they spotted Rosebud, clipboard in hand, directing the florist who had arrived with several dozen pots of pink tulips. "Harvey, I'm relieved you're here. I've been trying to make certain that I'm following your directions. Marty's in the kitchen going over things with the caterers."

"I'll take the teapots to the kitchen," Enid said eagerly. "I'll be back."

As she walked away, Rosebud said, "Harvey, I wasn't certain what you meant with the notes you wrote about Table 20. Will you please check that for me?"

As he walked into the room, Frank was looking around. "Is there something you would like me to take care of, Rosebud?" Frank asked hopefully. "With all these women scurrying around, I'm beginning to feel out of place."

"Would you mind going out to the parking lot and waiting for the harpist, Frank? I'm certain she'll need help getting her harp in the building and up onto the stage," Rosebud suggested.

Just then Ellie May came running into the dining room, carrying several trays of cookies. Huffing and puffing a bit, she said, "My goodness, look at those tulips. Those large pots along the front of the stage are absolutely gorgeous. And, the tables…I think they're even nicer than they were last year." As she spotted the pink napkins neatly arranged at each table, she moved into her investigative mood. Even though Rebecca had reported that it appeared the problem had ceased, she needed to be on her toes since pink was one of the preferred colors of the napkin thief. Everyone knows that a leopard doesn't change his spots.

Celeste, who had just finished putting programs on every chair, said, "I'll take those trays back to the kitchen, Ellie May. By the way, William was here earlier and he has the stage all set up for the entertainment. I'm looking forward to hearing our new chorus. I just may have to take one of these cookies off the tray. After all, we must be certain that all the food we're serving is tasty," Celeste teased as she hurried away with the goodies.

Harvey checked Table 20 and then he double-checked all the assigned tables to make certain that his directions had been followed. "Rosebud, you and your helpers did a great job setting up the tables. Everything looks perfect," Harvey said happily.

"Stretch chased me out of the kitchen," Enid said as she rejoined the others. "He told me that this was not his *first rodeo*. I thought it might have something to do with a large picture of his horse that was hanging on the kitchen wall. I had to ask Frank what that saying meant and they all had a good laugh. Anyway, here I am. I'm getting a bit nervous about my solo," Enid said. "I'm glad that I'll sing before Abigail. She's so good and I'm just…"

"I heard you sing, Enid. You have nothing to worry about. The ladies will love you," Rosebud said.

"Wow, this place looks great!" Harry said, as he came through the doorway with several cameras slung over his shoulders. "Enid, taking the pictures of your teapots at this event was a super idea. The colors will be fantastic."

"Celeste requested that we also get shots of the other activities for her scrapbook," Rosebud reminded Harry.

"I hear that Representative Kelly Moore is the speaker," Harry said. "I had the pleasure of meeting her last month at a meeting of the Bankers Association. And, I understand that she's very partial to the charity you chose this year. In fact, she has done several TV spots designed to increase donations to the *Mothers and Babies Fund.*

"Harry, when you take the photos of the ladies using my teapots, must we get them to sign a release like we do for other events?" Enid questioned.

"Yes. I brought plenty of forms with me and I'll make sure that I get their signatures. If there are particular ladies that you would like me to include, just let me know," Harry said.

"Since over a dozen women from the community have also registered for the tea, there will be lots of women that I don't know, but because this is a charity event, I think we should include some of them, too," Enid suggested.

"Well, Rosebud, everything looks great. Will Phillip be here?" Harvey asked.

"No. I want to say that this isn't his cup of tea, but I don't dare," Rosebud said as she laughed. "However, he did send along a donation."

When Nigel heard this, he pursed his lips and rolled his eyes. He obviously hadn't changed his mind about the retired doctor. But he was pleased that Phillip wouldn't be attending the tea—at least Nigel didn't have to look at the man. While Nigel knew full well that Rosebud had never been committed to him, he used to think that she might change her attitude. But now—now that he'd met Enid—his outlook had become more positive.

Mary Beth entered the dining room and took her seat at the registration desk promptly at one-thirty. Other than manning the registration desk at Morning Glory Hill, this was her favorite assignment. Proud of her straw hat with rosebuds around the crown, and the light pink, cotton party dress that she had ordered online, she felt prettier than ever. She relished welcoming each person—most of them she knew personally. Just as the first guest arrived, the harpist began playing.

Harry watched the women as they entered. Of course, he knew that Sally would be the first one in the door and he chuckled as he watched her try to hang on to her very large straw hat as she pushed her way to the exact table she wanted. He felt that this event could be taken for a fashion show since the ladies were wearing hats to compliment their flowery cotton dresses. It was going to be difficult to choose which ones to photograph for Enid's book. He took a seat in the back of the dining room and waited for the party to begin.

The decibel level rose distinctively when Representative Kelly Moore entered the room. With Marty by her side, she greeted many of the women as they made their way to the center table. Marty then approached the microphone and the audience quieted down.

"Welcome to the second annual *Tip Toe Thru the Tulips Tea*. As you are aware, today is a charity event with our proceeds going to the *Mothers and Babies Fund*, a group dedicated to helping women make the right choices for themselves and their babies. Our guest speaker today, Representative Kelly Moore, is the special spokesperson for this organization. I feel that Representative Kelly Moore is the little engine that could because she has fought an uphill battle in helping this group get established and proving itself to be an invaluable asset to women and their babies. It is a great pleasure for me to introduce Representative Kelly Moore," Marty said as she moved aside and turned the podium over to the politician who received a warm welcome.

Kelly held the audience's attention for about thirty minutes. Her speech was informative, poignant, dynamic, and sometimes humorous. Moore demonstrated a confident demeanor. The women were inspired, especially Enid. For a woman who wasn't that much younger than Enid, she had a great attitude. Something clicked inside Enid—maybe she, too, could be more spirited and active. After all, look how her idea of using the teapots at the bazaar was so readily accepted and appreciated by Marty and the others—and, perhaps, in her own little way, add verve and punch to her new life at MGH. It was a thought worth considering. When

Moore completed her presentation, the audience gave her a standing ovation.

As the servers made their appearance, they were carefully pushing carts loaded with beautiful teapots. Enid was trying to keep track of where each pot was being placed. She was thrilled to hear so many compliments. Just then, Marty picked up the microphone and said, "Ladies, I was remiss earlier. Many of the teapots you see on your tables are from Enid Murphy's beautiful collection. Please give her a hand for allowing us to have the pleasure of using her prized china. Also, Harry Hamilton will be coming around to take some photos that Enid plans on using for a book she's creating for the *Harvest Moon Bazaar*. Meanwhile, enjoy the tea and goodies.

Marty spotted William who was standing behind the curtain waving frantically. She suddenly realized that he wanted her to inform the audience that the MGH chorus would be presenting a program for their enjoyment. "And for your listening pleasure, our in-house chorus will be making their debut in about thirty minutes."

Enid was surprised to see Julia sitting at one of the tables with three ladies Enid didn't recognize. While she was pleased to see her sister, she would wait a bit before walking over to greet her. Since her friends were with her, Enid was certain that Julia would be on her best behavior. Suddenly Enid became nervous when she thought about her solo. In order to get through it, Enid decided that she wouldn't look at Julia during her presentation. *Someday I might get enough backbone not to care what my sister thinks of me.* But then, she had always felt that Julia was smarter, prettier and more talented than she was. Enid wasn't certain that she would ever rid herself of this self-imposed baggage. However, the audience had clapped in appreciation when Marty *publicly* thanked her for the use of her teapots. Her friends, Harry and Harvey, had faith in her—maybe this is just the beginning.

When William walked across the stage—the cue for all those in the chorus to join him— Enid jumped up and headed for Catherine's table. "I'm here to drive your chariot," Enid said as she took hold of Catherine's wheelchair. 'I'll take you up the back ramp—hang on."

The chorus members took their places quickly. Abigail approached from the rear of the stage and stood next to William. Nigel moved to the microphone. "The members of the Morning Glory Chorus are pleased to present their very first program at this annual event. First, please give a hand to William Williams, our patient and talented director." After a short pause, Nigel went on to provide the audience with an overview of the program.

When the chorus sang *How Great Thou Art* the audience was spell-bound. For a split second, there was absolute silence. Then, suddenly, the audience responded with a standing ovation. Enid's shoulders seemed a bit higher when this happened. Then she stepped forward, and as she took her place alongside William, she took a quick breath. As Enid began to sing *Stormy Weather*, a story about unrequited love, all her feelings seemed to pour from her soul. The misery and heartbreak she was feeling resonated with the audience through her smoky, sultry rendition. No one was more surprised than Enid to hear the audience explode with thunderous applause

Nigel couldn't take his eyes off her. Enid had moved him. She had allowed herself to be vulnerable with that song—not knowing how it would be received. This woman—this woman who just took a bow—had all this talent hidden—but not any longer.

As Abigail exchanged places with Enid, you could hear a pin drop in the room. Abigail smiled at William and waited for her cue to begin her offering of *Love is a Many Splendid Thing*. Her well-trained voice resounded throughout the room. Once again, the audience demonstrated their approval with a standing ovation. Finally, for their last number, the chorus offered their interpretation of *Tip Toe Thru the Tulips*. When the program was over, many of the ladies made their way to the stage to congratulate the chorus members. Andt, as usual, Sally was the first one who made it to the stage.

Nigel worked his way over to Enid. "You were fantastic," he said in a surprisingly timid tone. "Enid, I had no idea that you had such a beautiful voice. Wow. I got chills up and down my spine when you sang. I hope we won't have to wait too long to hear you again."

"Thank you, Nigel. How nice of you to say that," Enid replied.

"By the way, you look great, too," Nigel said as he was already scolding himself for not thinking of a better word than *great*.

"Thank you, again," a blushing Enid replied.

As the two of them approached the stage steps, Nigel took Enid's arm and guided her descent. Enid didn't fail to notice his gesture. Smiling, and with her new knowledge, she had not only seen Nigel in a different, somewhat enchanting light, she had found enough courage to walk over to her sister and face whatever her sister would say or do.

As she neared Julia's table, she was devastated when she saw her sister stand up and hurry away. Nigel was watching. He couldn't believe that Julia had done something that despicable. He quickly reached for Enid's hand, and said, "Enid, let's you and I go for a stroll. If you get chilly, I'll give you my jacket." She squeezed his hand and allowed him to lead her out of the building.

As the guests filed out of the dining room, Ellie May stood beside the door, trying hard not to look conspicuous. She greeted most of them by name and nodded politely to those whom she did not know. Her eyes looked over purses and any items that guests were carrying. She was disappointed that she hadn't spied any napkins. Her gut kept telling her that the napkin thief had struck again. If only she had known that not just one--or two--but three napkins had also left the dining room and that her gut had been right, she would have, at least, gotten some self-satisfaction.

CHAPTER 20

As Nigel approached *The Night Owl*, he was elated to see that Enid was already there with William. The three of them could probably be considered *regulars*. "Hi, fellow night owls," Nigel said cheerfully.

William pulled out a chair for his friend. "Hey, Jake," he called out, "you have another customer."

The swinging door to the kitchen opened and Jake hurried to take Nigel's order. "The other night I heard you say that you like sticky buns. Well, guess what? I just made a fresh batch. You want to try one?" Jake asked hopefully.

"OMG, do I? You bet your sweet a..." Nigel's eyes opened wide when he realized what he had almost said. Looking at Enid sheepishly, he said, "Oops, I forgot that we have a lady here."

Enid smiled. "Jake, I would love to have one of those buns, too."

"Coming right up. How about you, William?" Jake asked.

"Not tonight, Jake. I'm feeling like I'm not operating on all my burners," William replied.

"Buddy, what's happening?" Nigel asked.

"Just tired. I started a new exercise program and I believe I overdid it. I think I'm going to call it a night, folks," William said as he stood up. "I'll take a nice warm bath perhaps that will relieve these aching muscles."

"Need any help?" Nigel asked.

"Nah. Don't worry. I'll be fine in the morning," William said as he walked away.

As Nigel watched his best friend head for his apartment, he said, "I hope he's okay. He's a great guy. We've been friends ever since this place opened."

"I must say, Nigel, I had so much fun at the tea yesterday. It was a special occasion, and I got through my solo without fainting," Enid said.

"You were fantastic," Nigel said as he blushed a bit.

"Thank you, Nigel. I don't know what the chorus would do without William. He's not only a good musician, but an excellent director. And, Abigail…well she's as good as any of the professionals we hear on TV. Her voice is so clear and her pitch is perfect." Enid hesitated. Then she said, "Nigel, it was so sweet of you yesterday—you know, how concerned you were about me. I really appreciated that."

"Enid, do you mind if I ask you a personal question?" Nigel said.

"Ask away. We're friends," Enid said as she leaned forward.

"What's wrong with your sister? She insults everyone and most of the time she's grouchy," Nigel continued.

'She wasn't always like this. When we were kids, we did everything together. But when Julia was about sixteen or so, she began to change. She would be as happy as a lark one minute and then the next she would be irate. I thought things would get better when she married, but then I really think they got worse. I often wondered if she could be bipolar—I hear so much of that nowadays."

Nigel thought for a bit. "Maybe she has an unresolved problem that's eating away at her. I heard that on a Dr. Phil show the other day. Like, maybe someone hurt her, you know, maybe not sexually, but emotionally. Geez, listen to me…just like I know what I'm talking about," Nigel said just as Jake reappeared with their pastries.

"Oh, the aroma is wonderful," Enid said.

"I brought some butter in case you want some. Rebecca told me that locals like it that way. Enjoy!" Jake said as he returned to the kitchen.

The two of them were thoroughly enjoying their buns when Jake returned with a pot of hot coffee. "I just may never, ever leave this place, Jake. You're spoiling me," Nigel said.

"That would be fine with me. I could use some company here," Jake said. "Got to run, though. I have bread to make."

"You know, Nigel, you're amazing. You may have hit on something regarding Julia. I guess I gave up long ago trying to find out what was wrong with her, but you planted some seeds in this old brain. However, I was surprised to learn that she's made friends with Samuel. That puzzles me. What do you know about him?"

"Samuel's very intelligent. He teaches history at the university. He's also president of our Mayors Council. He can get things done, but he wants them done his way or not at all. He used to make unkind remarks about Harry and

Harvey, but that stopped when Harry won an award for his photograph of Oscar, Samuel's cat. As far as I know, he's not interested in the ladies," Nigel explained.

They were quiet, enjoying the silence and the companionship while they sipped on their coffee.

"Nigel, your name reminds me of an English novel I read some time ago—can't remember the title. But, anyway, one of the characters in that book was named Nigel. How did you get such a romantic name?" Enid asked sweetly.

"Well, there's a story there. You see, when I was born, the family couldn't agree on a name for me. So they decided that they would each write the name they wanted on a slip of paper and they put all the slips into a hat. My mom pulled one out. That's how I got my real name which is **six and seven-eighths**," Nigel said as his cheeks puffed with laughter.

For a few seconds, Enid was quiet. Then she burst out laughing. "Nigel, you are so funny—you are a breath of fresh air," she said as she gently tapped his hand.

She could not have made Nigel any happier.

CHAPTER 21

"Okay, folks, let's get started," Frank said as he faced about a dozen residents in the meeting room. "Since you all have reserved seats on the bus we're taking to the track tomorrow, there have been multiple requests to learn more about racing and the elements involved in betting, So, welcome to How to Bet on Horses, 101."

"I'd like to learn how not to lose," Nigel said kiddingly. "Teacher, will there be a test?"

"Your test will come tomorrow if you bet, As far as not losing is concerned, I can't guarantee anything. We're going to show our support for Stretch, whose horse, LUCKY LADY, is running in the sixth race. I can help you to understand how to bet. Winning, however, is another thing."

Catherine raised her hand. "Frank, if this wheelchair is going to get in the way at the track, I better not go along."

"No problem, Catherine. We'll take you up to the dining room in the elevator. Our group has reservations in the clubhouse for lunch. And, to make it easier for those of you who will be betting, my daughters are going along and they will act as our runners," Frank explained. "They will check with each one of you, go over your betting slips, and they'll go to the windows and get your tickets. And, for those of you who are winners, they'll cash your tickets and deliver the money to your table."

"What happens if I hit a really big, big ticket?" Nigel asked as he rubbed his hands together.

Frank laughed. "Then you'll have to go to the window and sign for your money. But, let's learn the basic rules of betting first." Frank pulled a large portable chalkboard to the front of the meeting room. Across the board, he wrote WIN PLACE SHOW. "*Win* is just that—the horse must be the first one to cross the finish line. If you bet *place*, then your horse must either be first or second in the race. And, last, if you bet *show*, then your horse must come in either first or second, or just third. A single ticket costs two dollars."

Rosebud wrinkled up her nose. "It all sounds so complicated. I'm confused."

"Once you observe one or two races, Rosebud, the clouds will disappear. When you see the tote board—"

"What's a tote board?" Celeste asked.

"A *tote board* is the big electronic board that informs the bettors about what action is taking place on each horse. And, it will show what the winning tickets will pay. Honestly, folks it won't take you long to feel at home with what's going on at the track," Frank said, trying to reassure his friends.

"Frank, a friend of mine talks about betting a horse across the board. What does that mean?" Nigel asked.

"*Across the board* means that you want to purchase a ticket on a horse for all three spots. That costs six dollars. If the horse wins, you get paid for *win, place* and *show*. If the horse comes in second, you get paid for *place* and *show*. If the horse is third, you only get paid for *show*." Frank waited for a few seconds, and then he asked, "Questions?"

"How much do you win on a two dollar bet?" Celeste asked.

"That depends on the odds. The betting public creates the odds. For instance, if lots of people bet on one horse, then the odds go down—you get paid less. But when only a few people bet on a horse, the odds go up—you win more money if that horse wins."

"Let me get this straight. If I play LUCKY LADY across the board and she wins, then I get paid for my *win* ticket, my *place* ticket **and** my *show* ticket?" Ellie May asked as she pulled her eyebrows together. "And, that will only cost me six dollars?"

"You got it, Ellie May," Frank said.

"Frank, can you explain some of the so-called exotic bets? I hear that's where the big payoffs can happen," Gordon stated.

"A typical lawyer," Nigel teased. "He wants the big bucks."

Gordon just smiled and replied, "Be careful, my friend. I tell you what, Nigel—how about you and I having a side bet. Let's say fifty dollars. Frank can hold the money and whoever wins the most, between the two of us, gets the pot. What do you say?"

"You're on. I have always wanted to take a lawyer down," Nigel said as he got his wallet out. "Here's my fifty, Frank. Now, Mr. Lawyer, let's see you put your fifty in the pot."

Gordon pulled out his wallet. Pretending that he was leafing through lots of bills, Gordon said, "I don't know if I have something as small as a fifty."

"Gordon, for heaven's sake. You barely have any money in there," Marie said as she poked his arm. "You two will have spent all your money before we even get to the track." As Gordon handed Frank a fifty, Marie said, "Now, Frank, please continue."

"*Exactas* allow you to bet on the horses that will come in first and second for two dollars. These pay more but the horses must come in first and second. But, for four dollars, you can *box* them, which means that it doesn't matter which one is first and which is second. A *trifecta* is when you are betting on the horses that will come in first, second, and third and it costs two dollars. These usually have nice payoffs, but they are hard to hit. However, for six dollars, you can *box* the three horses and then it doesn't matter which is first, second, or third. While this is considered a better bet—because it is a reduced cost—you also receive a reduce payout."

"That sounds hard," Catherine said.

"Yes, it is. Listen, folks. If you decide you want to try an exotic bet tomorrow, just flag me down and I'll help you. If LUCKY LADY wins, Stretch wants all of us in Winner's Circle when the picture is taken. So, our main goal is to root for her. However, if we win a little money along the way, that will be okay, too," Frank said pleasantly.

Frank then handed out some printed materials for the residents to take along. Catherine turned to Enid and said,

"I'm so glad that you're going along. I still feel that I'm such a bother with my wheelchair."

"Catherine, you're going to love it. And, if Stretch's horse wins, it will be even more exciting." Enid said reassuringly.

As the meeting was breaking up, Nigel said to Catherine and Enid, "I'm headed out to lunch at *The Texas Steak House*. Would you ladies like to come along as my guests?" he asked hopefully.

"But my chair—" Catherine said.

"I can handle that. Meanwhile, I have an advanced copy of *The Daily Racing Form* which means we can look over the horses that are running tomorrow. Who knows what the three of us can figure out?" Nigel began pushing Catherine's chair with one hand, and with the other, he was brave enough to take Enid's.

CHAPTER 22

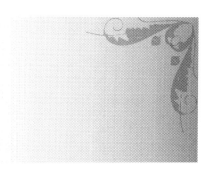

The Square was extremely noisy. The seventeen people waiting for the bus to go to the track all seemed to be talking at the same time. Frank was trying to count noses to make certain that everyone was there before he would make his announcements.

Barry Adams, came running across *The Square* calling out for Frank. "I'm going with you. Mary Beth offered to supervise my other activities. We felt that you might need extra help to manage Catherine."

"Glad to have you along, Barry. Folks, may I have your attention, please. When we arrive at the track, please go through the doorway on the far right and wait there. We'll have to get Catherine off the lift and up to the doorway and that will take a few minutes. Then, we'll take the elevator to the clubhouse which is on the third floor, where a hostess will direct us to our tables. Any questions?" Frank asked as he continued to count heads.

Nigel raised his hand. "Frank, isn't Stretch going along?"

"Oh, he left some time ago. He's probably on the backside talking with LUCKY LADY," Frank said as he smiled broadly. "Nigel, you look like a track regular in your jacket with lots of pockets for tickets, your racing paper under your arm, and your binoculars hanging around your neck."

"I have a question," Rosebud said. "Is it okay if we bet on the other races—you know—the ones before LUCKY LADY runs?"

"Of course. Just let my daughters know what you want to play and they'll help you. They'll also explain how to fill out your betting slips. This service is for all of you who do not want to go to the windows yourselves. For those of you who want to place your own bets, remember to use the right order—mention the name of the track, then the race number, then the amount of the bet, then the type of bet you want, and finally the number of the horse not the horse's name. Make certain that you know all that before you go to the seller's window. It may sound complicated, but if you use the betting slips you'll find on the tables, you won't have any problems."

"But why must we say the track name?" Celeste asked. "After all, we're at the track."

"The track accepts bets on races being held at other tracks across the country. For instance, someone might want to play a horse running at Belmont, or Aqueduct, or Santa Anita. You'll see some of these races on the screens all around the clubhouse as well as on the screens at your tables. That was a good question, Celeste."

Catherine leaned over to Enid and said, "I'm not sure that I can do all this. It is *so* confusing."

"Don't worry, Catherine. Nigel and I will help you. Barry's here, too, so you have nothing to worry about. This will be fun. Just relax," Enid said as she patted Catherine's hand.

"Here's the bus," Frank announced.

Before Frank could even turn around, Sally flew by him and headed for the bus. Frank took Marty's hand and they quietly followed the stocky woman to the bus.

Just then Julia appeared. "Enid, you're not going to the racetrack, are you?"

"You *bet* I am," Enid said playfully as she realized her intentional pun.

"Another losing financial dealing." Julia said as she wagged her finger at her sister.

"We'll see, Julia—we'll see," Enid responded as she took charge of Catherine's wheelchair and walked away.

On the drive to the track, Nigel was studying *The Daily Racing Form* as if he knew what he was reading. "Enid, in the first race there's a horse named *FABULOUS DANCER*. I will bet on that one. Hey, William," he said as he tapped his friend's shoulder, "look at this horse," as he handed William the newspaper.

"Go for it, Nigel. The name is definitely you. But I really don't know what all these other figures are. You'll have to ask Frank."

Nigel then spent time with Frank, who patiently explained some of the statistics to him.

"Just remember, Nigel, betting on the horses is a form of gambling. But, it can be fun if you're careful with how you bet and how much you're willing to lose," Frank cautioned.

Before too long, the excited group found themselves in the roomy elevator on their way to the clubhouse. A pleasant young woman met them as they stepped off the elevator and led them to their reserved tables.

"Miss, I saw that there are two more floors in this building. What goes on there?" Gordon asked.

"The fourth floor is our night club and the fifth floor is reserved for owners of horses that run here at the track," she explained. As soon as they were all seated, Frank's daughters began circulating and explaining the process involved in filling out the betting slips.

"Oh, Enid, look—we can see the whole track from here. Look at the tote board—the numbers keep changing just like Frank said they would," Catherine said.

"I'm going to the window to get my ticket on FABULOUS DANCER. Are you two going to bet on this race?" Nigel asked.

"I think I'll just watch this one," Enid said. "I'll take a chance in the next one."

"Me, too," Catherine said.

When Nigel returned, he showed Enid his ticket. "My horse is number four and I played it across the board."

"I know what that means," Catherine said proudly. "Win, place and show!"

"Look, Nigel, your horse is so pretty," Enid said.

"No, not pretty—*handsome* is the right word. He's a colt—a male," Nigel said.

Catherine and Enid laughed.

"I'm glad I brought my binoculars," Nigel said as he adjusted his glasses. "Now I can watch him just like I'm right beside him."

"They're off!" the track announcer shouted.

On the far turn, Nigel's horse, started moving out. Enid and Catherine were both shouting for the horse as he came down the stretch run three lengths in front of all the other horses.

"You won!" they both yelled at Nigel, who was still watching the horse with his binoculars.

When the numbers were posted, and the prices appeared, Nigel was thrilled. Nigel quickly added them together and said, "Ladies, I just won sixty-two fifty! Thanks for your help. Drinks are on me." Nigel stood and yelled to Gordon, "Get ready to lose that fifty!"

Everyone congratulated Nigel, on his win and he felt like a king.

Nigel's success inspired the others to place bets and the fun was on. After the fifth race, Frank met with his group to explain that they needed to make their bets on LUCKY LADY early since they were all going down to the Winner's Circle in case she won.

"Here's our plan. Make sure you pay your luncheon bill and get your betting slips completed for the sixth race. We'll then go down to the track level and be in walking distance of the Winner's Circle. If she wins, Stretch wants all of us to be in the photo. Any questions?" Frank asked.

As the horses for the sixth race appeared on the track for the post parade, the MGH group was lined up along the fence. Just then, Harvey joined his friends and said, "I've been looking for you guys. Harry's around here somewhere with his cameras. Oh, here he comes now."

After getting the group to turn around, Harry snapped a few shots of the excited group. "I'll have to get permission to take some inside the Winner's Circle and I sure hope I get it. This has been an unbelievable experience for me."

"I had no idea that horses were so large!" Catherine said as she watched them prepare for the race. "Oh, look at LUCKY LADY! Her tail is braided and little morning glories are entwined. She's so beautiful."

Jose Amigo, the jockey, was wearing bright pink silks. His shirt had morning glories embroidered across the back, a special design that Stretch had created.

Suddenly, Stretch was right behind them. "What do you think?" he asked unable to hide his nervousness.

"She looks like a winner, Stretch," Frank said.

One by one, the members of the group talked to Stretch. "Remember, she comes from behind, so she won't be upfront at first. Keep your eyes on the far turn. She should begin to make her move then. When she nears her last turn to come down the stretch, she'll make her big move and—if she's fine—that will be *goodbye Charlie!*"

"What does that mean?" Rosebud asked.

"That means no one will catch her," Stretch said confidently.

Since Catherine was in her wheelchair, she wasn't able to see the backstretch. So, she decided that she would close her eyes and just listen to the track announcer. She heard the racket as the jockeys guided their horses into the gate and the gatekeepers made certain that each horse was secure. Then she heard a bell.

"They're off...SPIDER WEB jumped out followed by MISS POLLY...MAMA BEAR is a close third..." Catherine wasn't interested in the rest until he said "And LUCKY

LADY is trailing." Catherine's heart skipped a beat. She waited until he boomed, "Here they come down the stretch…MAMA BEAR is first, followed by RED UPSET with LUCKY LADY closing fast on the outside." Catherine repeated over and over, *come on girl, come on girl, you can do it.* "And it's LUC KY LADY first, MAMA BEAR second, and RED UPSET third."

The MGH group went wild. They were jumping up and down, hugging one another, and waving their winning tickets in the air. They watched excitedly as Jose, who blessed himself, returned with the winning horse. He skillfully guided LUCKY LADY into the Winner's Circle.

Stretch yelled for the group to come inside, and one by one, they timidly entered this special area. Stretch patted his horse on her nose. The horse picked up her ears and nudged Stretch. She could smell that hidden under his jacket were two apples—her favorite treat.

"Not yet, LUCKY. After you're dried and settled in your stall, you'll get the apples," Stretch said like a proud father. Stretch made certain to congratulate the jockey and the trainer. They both had contributed a great deal to the win.

Harry hurried over to the track photographer and got permission to take a picture. He not only got a shot of the jockey on the horse, but he was able to get a great shot when Stretch shook the jockey's hand.

Frank ushered the group out of the Winner's Circle and said, "Okay, folks, follow me and I'll show you where you can cash your tickets. You deserve to have the privilege of doing that yourselves," Frank instructed as he lead his little band of happy winners to the cashier's cage. As they headed for the bus, Frank said, "By the way, I have one hundred dollars in my wallet that goes to either Gordon or Nigel. Which one gets it?"

"I hate to admit it, but Nigel won more than I," Gordon said regretfully.

"Thanks, Gordon. Any time you want a rematch, just call me," Nigel said as he stuffed the money in his pocket.

The bus ride home was even noisier than it was on the way to the track. Everyone had stories to tell.

"This has been a perfect afternoon. Stretch is walking on air. The racing game is not an easy one, so I'm delighted that he's had such good luck. However, Stretch told me that his trainer is moving to Belmont Park and LUCKY LADY will be going with him."

"Oh, no. Then we won't get to see her again," Abigail said sadly. "Why are they moving?"

"Bigger purses and more opportunities for the horse. Racing is a very expensive hobby so Stretch must make the right decisions if he wants to stay in the game," Frank responded.

"Well, LUCKY LADY will always be ours!" Nigel said proudly. "Frank, I've got an idea. Do you think we could form an owners' group, each one kicking in some money, and buy a horse?"

Frank laughed. Shaking his head, he said, "Nigel, we're all too old to get involved in something that risky. It's an intriguing idea, but one that would be filled with tremendous pressure. Tell you what—we could set up our own little track at MGH. We could build some wooden horses and race them just for fun."

"How do you race wooden horses?" Nigel asked.

"You use a large cage with three dice. Let's say we have six horses. We shake the dice cage and the numbers are two, four and five. Well, that means the number two, four and five each move one spot. We did this once when we were raising funds for the fire company and it was well received," Frank said encouragingly.

"That sounds like fun. We'll get on that soon," Nigel said. "Barry, will you help us put something together?"

"Certainly, Nigel. And, you won't be breaking any rules, since you'll have the event for charity," Barry explained.

"Since when did Nigel worry about breaking any rules?" Gordon chided.

As the bus rolled along, the group began to settle in. Nigel, however, was busy sketching wooden horses.

CHAPTER 23

S amuel was killing time in his apartment by browsing online. He didn't want to be in *The Square* when the racetrack fans returned. He couldn't bear to be around Nigel and his silliness. His list of people he disliked at Morning Glory Hill was growing. Of course, he hated both Harry and Harvey Hamilton for certain. Ever since he was caught peering into their front window, hoping to see some kind of perverted sexual act going on, and using such evidence to get others to hate them too, instead, he was caught by a hidden camera that Harry had placed on their front porch. Of course, Harry had taken advantage of the situation by pretending he didn't know about Samuel's spying by producing that damned award-winning photograph of Oscar, Samuel's beloved Siamese cat. Samuel was willing to go along with the supposed friendship; that is, until it turned out not to be in his best interest.

Nigel, on the other hand, was not near as intelligent as Harry. In fact, Samuel thought of Nigel as a Neanderthal— way down on the human chain of development. Nigel would never be clever enough to discover Samuel's secret. The day that Nigel saw Julia and him getting off the elevator with their overnight bags, however, still annoyed Samuel. Well, if Nigel thought of anything, it certainly wouldn't come close to the truth. Nigel was simply stupid and Samuel hated stupid. Nigel's childish jokes only proved that he didn't have a brain at all—just like the scarecrow in The Wizard of Oz. Samuel chuckled. He could picture Nigel with straw jutting out of his arms and legs, singing *if I only had a brain.*

Suddenly he found exactly what he had been searching for. There they were. All the things he had wanted. He also spied something that he felt that Julia would like. He clicked on that item, too. Putting his credit card numbers in carefully, Samuel sat back and sighed heavily. He even paid for two-day delivery—he felt like a kid in a candy store. All thoughts of Nigel had disappeared.

CHAPTER 24

Frank and Nigel were hunched over a workbench in the woodworking shop. "I got these plans off the Internet," Frank said. "They are fairly close to the ones I made a long time ago. What do you think?"

"I have to rely on your judgement, Frank. You're the woodworker. How many do you think we'll need?" Nigel asked. As he took another look at the blueprints, Nigel said, "What size will be right for us?

"To make our race interesting, we should have six horses. I think the horses should be about three feet high. They need a knob, or handle, on the top so that the jockeys can easily move them. We can't make them too heavy, but they also must be sturdy so they don't fall over," Frank explained.

"Six? Sounds like a lot of work," Nigel said.

"Nah, it won't take long. But getting the horses painted and decorated for the race will take time. After we make the horses, we'll auction them off to the highest bidder. Those bidders will then own the horses. They will have to name their horse, paint it, and/or decorate it in any way they please, and enter it in the Morning Glory Hill Derby,"

Frank said as he began calculating how much wood they would need.

"At the racetrack, the owners win money if their horse wins. What will our owners win?" Nigel asked.

"They will get whatever the auction of the horses brings in. Let's say, maybe a couple of hundred or so," Frank explained.

"Where are we gonna race them?" Nigel asked.

"We can put down chalk lanes on the rear lawn. The area next to the gazebo should work out fine. The first rain will wash the chalk lines away, so Hortense won't mind," Frank said reassuringly.

"How about the residents who don't have a horse in the race. How do we get them involved?" Nigel asked. "You know Hortense will want something to go to charity."

"They can bet on the horses. Tickets will be ten dollars. We will pay for *win only* to make it simple. Say we take in two thousand—we'll then divide the number of win tickets into that amount and that's what a win ticket will pay," Frank said. "I'm sure Gordon and William would take care of selling the tickets and the payoffs. As far as charity is concerned, we could allocate one half of what the auction produces and one half of what the selling of tickets brings in to a charity of Hortense's choice. How does that sound?"

"That's a smart idea. That way she'll have a part in making the event successful. This whole idea sounds like it will be fun. You know, we can call it Derby Day at MGH. We can even sell mint julips! Oh, and we'll get the ladies to wear their hats—they like to wear them. We better recruit

Harvey. He's a genius at bringing life to any event," Nigel said excitedly.

"Let's visit Hortense to make sure we can do all of this and then we'll take off for the lumber yard," Frank said as he folded up the blueprints and put them in his breast pocket.

"I think we should stop by for Harvey. I hear he's a genius at negotiating with vendors and we just may need his expertise," Nigel suggested.

"Nigel, I know how to buy wood. We'll get Harvey involved shortly. Meanwhile, I'm the boss of the workshop," Frank said firmly.

Nigel shook his head in agreement. He wasn't about to argue with Frank. One thing Nigel learned a long time ago was that it was better to be second-in-command—that way, when anything went wrong, he could always maintain that he was merely following orders. Meanwhile, Enid knew that the idea of racing at MGH was all his idea. She had watched him sketching horses on the trip home from the racetrack. While Frank was a necessary part of putting it all together, it was still Nigel's brainstorm.

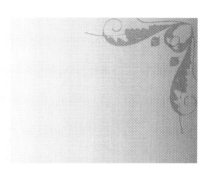

CHAPTER 25

Samuel rapped his gavel hard to indicate that he was ready to begin the meeting of The Mayors Council. "Folks, quiet, please. We need to get started. First, it is my pleasure to welcome Trixie and Benjamin Althouse, the newest residents of Morning Glory Hill. I'm pleased to say that I have known this couple for some time now through my association with the university. Ben, a native Californian, was Dean of the math department; Trixie, is well known as an author of children's books." Samuel waited while the group applauded.

"From the conversation that I heard before I started the meeting, I know that you're aware of Derby Day at MGH. Nigel has prepared handouts regarding the particulars of this event, and I encourage all of you to get involved. The proceeds of the event will be donated to our local food bank which, as you probably know, we have supported several times in the past. So, if you have any questions, please see Nigel after the meeting. Now, let's get started on the agenda for today," Samuel said in an authoritative voice.

Out of the corner of his eye, Samuel could see that Harvey and Nigel—two from his dislike list—were whispering back and forth. However, he was not going to give them the satisfaction of knowing that they were annoying him. But, just to prove his authority, Samuel rapped the gavel one more time.

"Hortense has a few items that she would like to share with the Council. Hortense, the floor is yours," Samuel said.

"Let me welcome the Althouses one more time," she said as she motioned toward the couple. "Ben reminded me that he prefers to be called <u>Ben</u>. I am certain that you will enjoy being part of our extended family. Now, I must report that there will be an increase in the rental fees at your next sign-up time. The amount of the increase will be dependent on the type of apartment that you occupy. This increase was necessary due to higher electrical costs as well as additional landscaping. I'm pleased to report though, that since we have had the cameras installed in the garage area, our insurance rates have been reduced," Hortense said as she smiled.

"I'm not certain that all of you know about the two storage areas in the garage and what they're for. One area is strictly for maintenance to store all types of tools and equipment. The other room is for residents to temporarily store items that they can't use in their apartments. Remember, I said *temporarily*. After an item has been stored in this area for longer than six months. the resident will be notified that if the item is not removed within thirty days, we will dispose of the item. If you receive such a notice, please make a decision immediately regarding what you want to do with that item. I'll be happy to work with you on disposal plans. Thanks for your attention. Thank you, Samuel, for permission to attend this meeting today," Hortense said courteously.

Samuel was almost speechless with this unexpected news. He had to intervene with matters regarding the resident storage room. Taking a deep breath, Samuel turned to Hortense. "I would like to volunteer to be the intermediary if any actions need to be taken for items in the resident storage room. I would be willing to work with any resident in getting rid of unwanted items. I think if we keep this area under the direction of the residents themselves, we can work together to obtain the best results for everyone involved. And, since I have access to several organizations that might be interested in some of the items, we might be able to make a few dollars for our benefit fund," Samuel said as he nervously rustled through his paperwork.

"How gracious of you, Samuel. I'm more than willing to turn that room over to you. You're such an organized person. That's one less thing that I won't need to worry about. Thank you so much," Hortense said as she left the meeting room.

Samuel went through the rest of the agenda in a mechanical fashion. His nerves were settling down. Now that he would have the final say of what happened to items in the resident storage room, he had time to protect the turf that he wanted to keep as his own. He finally looked at Julia. She gently shook her head up and down—they were on the same page.

The meeting room had cleared out quickly—all except Catherine. She was sitting in the back row looking befuddled. Her breathing had quickened as she tried to determine where she was. Enid suddenly popped back into the room, looking for her cell phone. When she spied Catherine, she knew immediately that something was wrong.

"Catherine, are you waiting for someone?" she asked tenderly.

Catherine looked at her for a few seconds. "I don't think so." Then she looked around the room furtively. "I'm lost. Can you help me?"

CHAPTER 26

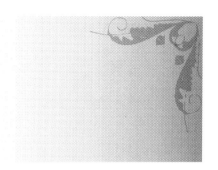

Marty was meeting with Harvey in his apartment to look over the sketches he made of how the dining room could be decorated and arranged for the wedding.

"How's Frank taking all of this?" Harvey asked.

"He says he doesn't know anything about planning weddings. Personally, I think he's a bit nervous, so he's thrown himself into planning Derby Day so he has an excuse for not helping. I'm fine with it, though. He did look over the invitations and he made one suggestion that I readily used. We chose the first Saturday in September for the date. I keep in touch with his girls so they can give me advice and counsel. They want dancing so they felt a late time, like six, would be best for the ceremony. You know, I wanted to keep it as simple as possible, but it seems to be taking on a life of its own," Marty said happily.

"Here are two ideas for how we can set up the dining room," Harvey said as he placed the sketches in front of Marty. "On this one, the wedding party will walk in through the front door and the lectern will be located right there where you see the X. On the second sketch, the wedding party will come in from the side door, and the minister will be located at the same spot as the first diagram indicates. The second idea will give us more room for flowers and decorations in the background as you walk down the aisle," Harvey said as he leaned forward to mark where the aisle would be.

"Oh, Harvey, you're fantastic. I love the idea of using lots of flowers. You know, when the bride is young and beautiful, maybe you don't need any flowers," Marty said as she laughed.

"I have the tables arranged so that everyone in the room will be able to see the procession. And, of course, the bridal party, which is very large, will form a semi-circle in front of the stage. Now, the pink circles indicate where we'll have flowers, and the green triangles indicate where we'll have shrubbery. Do you want to choose the flowers and shrubs, or are you leaving that up to the florist?"

"I would like to have Marie help me select them. She's so good at choosing colors and forms. Oh, Harvey, do you usually do that? I didn't mean to imply that—"

"I could do that, but this is your wedding. Perhaps Marie, you and I as a group could meet with the florist. How does that sound?" Harvey tactfully recommended.

"That's a great idea. Harvey, I guess I've already told you that we don't want a typical wedding cake. We thought that, if we had trays of various desserts, each guest could chose the one that they really like the best. What do you think?"

"I've seen that done several times. It's your wedding, my dear, and whatever you want you may have," Harvey said as he pulled out sketches of flowers and fountains.

"Now you sound just like Frank," Marty said laughingly. "I don't want to be a bridezilla."

"These," Harvey said as he pointed to more sketches, "can be expanded or cut back as you see fit."

"Oh, my, I love these," Marty said as she pulled out two of the sketches. "Can we do both of these?"

"You got it. Now, how about gifts?"

"Our invitation specifies that we don't want gifts. If guests chose to, they may make a donation to a charity of their choosing."

"Marty, you should have some place, however, where guests may leave gifts. You know, there are bound to be those who may have something very special that they want to give to the two of you. So, we could put a small table near the front entrance, so guests don't feel awkward walking around with something in their hands. We'll just let the table blend into the background," Harvey explained.

"Harvey, thank goodness I have you and Marie. I never thought I would need an event planner at my age!" Marty said. "By the way, this afternoon at two the horses for Derby Day are going to be auctioned off in *The Square*."

"Harry's all hyped up about the race. He plans on getting a horse. The way he talks, you would think they are live horses."

"Thanks again, Harvey. Would Friday morning be okay for you to go with us to the florist?" Marty said, still feeling a bit nervous about how she had handled this problem before.

"I'll call them and set that up, Marty. I'll do the driving."

"Harvey, I have an idea. How about we combine the wedding and Derby Day? I can ride in on one of the horses," Marty deadpanned.

In mocked seriousness, Harvey replied, "No way. I know I said *anything* you wanted, but you will *not* come down the aisle on a horse!"

CHAPTER 27

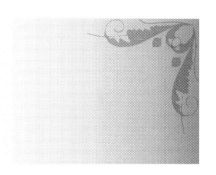

The Square was filled to overflowing. Frank had created a circle of folding chairs in the center of the room for those residents who wanted to bid on the horses. He had posted the rules and regulations for buying a horse: Only cash will be accepted. The owner will be responsible for decorating and naming the horse. The owner will serve as the jockey for the horse on Derby Day. The wooden horses were lined up in front of the reception desk with tags that were numbered from one to six.

Only five seats were occupied in the owners' circle—William, Nigel, Gordon, Harry and Rosebud. Frank was getting worried. He didn't want to buy a horse since he had enough responsibility in running the entire event.

Ben, the newest resident of Morning Glory Hill, approached Frank and said, "I'd like to participate in the bidding, but I was hanging back since I didn't want to take someone's place who had been a resident here much longer than I."

"Join us, Ben. We're glad that you want to be part of Derby Day," Frank said as he starting breathing a bit easier. "Okay, folks, we're ready to begin."

"Frank, we've been talking about the auction process. We feel that it might be better if we could all agree on one price and that would eliminate the need for bidding. Give us a minute to speak with Ben in private," Gordon said as the six formed a tight little group. After only a few minutes, Gordon said, "Frank, we have an offer for you. We understand that half of the total amount we pay for the horses will go to the owner of the winning horse, while the other half will go to the food bank. All of us have agreed to pay five hundred dollars for our horse. Will that be acceptable?"

The residents stood up and clapped.

"That's a fine offer. Since this is our first venture into the racing game, I think the residents are pleased with your offer. Each of you will draw a number from this bag to determine the post position for your horse. After you draw the number, give us your horse's name for the records," Frank said as the voice level of the spectators rose as they discussed the proceedings. "When you have chosen your number, you may claim your horse. Gentlemen, we'll let the lady draw first," Frank said as he walked over to Rosebud, who was waving at the spectators.

Someone in the crowd yelled, "Go, Rosebud, go!"

As she held up the number she drew, Frank said, "Rosebud, your horse will be Number Four. What's the name of your horse?"

"First, my horse is a filly and her name is RAVISHING ROSIE."

The audience laughed approvingly.

Our new resident, Ben, may draw next."

Rather timidly, Ben stood up and reached deep into the bag and pulled out Number Two.

"Ben, what is the name of your horse?"

"BIG BAD BEN," Ben replied.

"Now, our talented pianist is next."

William waved to Abigail and, with a flourish, he pulled out number one. "My horse is a filly, too," William said proudly. "Her name is LOVELY ABIGAIL."

Now the residents whooped and hollered while Abigail blushed.

"Gordon, draw your number," Frank directed.

Pretending that there were lots of numbers still in the bag, Gordon moved his hand around and around. "Ah, I think I found one," he said. "My horse's number is Five. Oh, and I am naming her BAHAMA MAMA."

"Now, for our photographer. We are down to two numbers. Pick one, Harry."

"Great, I picked Six. I get the outside post. You guys won't have a chance. My horse's name is PRETTY AS A PICTURE."

Nigel stood up. "I want to pick out of the bag, too."

"But there's only one number left," Frank argued.

"Placate me, Frank," Nigel said as he moved his hand around and around the inside of the bag. "Oh, look, my horse is Number Three!"

The audience applauded wildly.

"And, my horse's name will be FANCY DANCY."

"Owners, you may paint your horses and decorate them in any manner," Frank said, as he tried to sound like the announcer that he had heard at the track. "You may not insert any electrical devices to make them run faster. You may not use any performance enhancing drugs on your horse. You may only advance your horse during the race when the racing steward tells you to do so. You have two weeks to make your horse look like a winner. Hortense and two of her friends will be judging the horses for beauty. The winner will receive a certificate of beauty that will hang in our display case. However, the horse that wins the Derby will be on display in the case that is in the entryway. On Derby Day, we'll be selling **win tickets only** at ten dollars each at one o'clock and the horses must be in the gate and ready to run by two. Remember, the food bank will receive half of all the money that is bet on the race. I encourage you to be generous. Good luck, racing fans."

As people began to disband, Frank said, "Oh, just a minute, folks. I forgot something. We'll be collecting all the horses after the Derby, so that we can store them for next year. So, don't get too attached to them. They're only on loan to you. Next year, we'll clean them up and then you can start the decorating process all over again. Thanks to all of you!"

CHAPTER 28

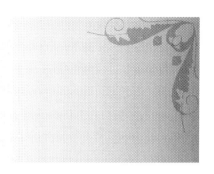

Nigel was anxious to begin working on his horse. He decided that FANCY DANCY needed to wear a tuxedo and a top hat for Derby Day. He rummaged through his closet and finally found the hat that he used to wear when he was in dance contests. He brushed the dust off the brim and plunked it on his head. As he admired himself in the mirror, he felt that he still had the charm and finesse that he had had when he was much younger. However, after taking a second look, he said out loud, "Well, maybe not."

He spread newspapers around his cement patio and put his horse right in the middle. He then painted the entire horse black. He would later use white paint for the horse's features. What he needed now was a large, bright red bow tie to add pizazz and glamour if he wanted to get the beauty certificate and win the race as well. He was shooting for the works. He decided that he wouldn't even tell Enid what he was doing with FANCY DANCY—he'd surprise her.

Nigel decided that, while the paint was drying, he would run over to the fabric store to buy the material he needed for the bow tie. Since it had to be large, he couldn't use one off the racks.

He felt out of place as soon as he entered the store. There were piles and piles of yard goods and rolls of every kind of fabric imaginable. He knew he needed help. Timidly, he approached a woman, who had a measuring tape draped around her neck and a small pin cushion strapped to her wrist. "Pardon, me, Miss, can you help me?" he asked.

She smiled broadly. She hadn't been called <u>Miss</u> in a long time. "Certainly, sir. What are you looking for?"

"To be honest, that's a tough question," Nigel said. "I have this wooden horse that I am going to put in a race at Morning Glory Hill, and I want to make a bow tie for him to wear."

The salesclerk pulled her eyebrows together. She had to refrain from laughing. But, she realized that she had never been asked to help dress a wooden horse. The man standing in front of her had such a great smile on his face, that he immediately won her over. "You want to make a bow tie? Why don't you purchase one?"

"I want a large tie…maybe eight or nine inches wide," Nigel explained as if it was not an unusual request.

"Oh, I see. Come with me," she said as she led him to the rear of the store. "What color do you want?"

"Bright red."

She started digging in a large carton that held all kinds of fabric scraps. "Here we go," she said as she pulled out a long strip of bright red taffeta. "If we double this, it will hold its stiffness and stay perky. Would you want me to make a bow tie for you?"

"Wow! Could you do that?" Nigel asked. He was dumbfounded for a minute.

She whipped scissors out of her apron pocket, made a few cuts, flipped the material around a few times, and, in no time flat, she had created a dramatic bright red bow tie for FANCY DANCY. "I must caution you, however—don't put your hands on the inside of the bow tie, since I used several pins to hold it together."

"Thank you very, very much. How much do I owe you for all you have done?"

The salesclerk laughed. "Nothing, sir. The scraps in that box are free to anyone who can use them. I hope your horse wins." She shook Nigel's hand warmly. "Good luck!"

Nigel didn't remember walking out of the store. He felt as if his feet had never touched the floor. All of this had to be a lucky omen. He hurried back to his apartment and immediately went out onto the patio. He couldn't believe his eyes…FANCY DANCY was gone!

Then he noticed the envelope. He ripped it open.

I have kidnapped FANCY DANCY. Unless you meet the ransom, I will turn him into five pounds of saw dust. I will contact you tomorrow with my terms.

Have a nice day. Yours truly,
The Horse Whisperer

CHAPTER 29

"Slow down, Nigel, I can't understand a word you're saying," William said as he led Nigel to the sofa. "Sit down, catch your breath, and then we'll talk."

Abigail, who had been going through some sheet music, immediately stood up and hurried to the kitchen to get Nigel a glass of water. "Here, Nigel. Sip this slowly."

Nigel took a deep breath, and said, "FANCY DANCY has been kidnapped. Here," he said as he handed William the note left by the Horse Whisperer.

"Nigel. Nigel. Someone's playing a trick on you. They really won't turn your horse into saw dust," William said assuredly as he read the note the second time.

"How do you know that? You don't. How can I get my horse back?" Nigel said getting close to tears.

"First, relax. Go along with this prank. Have fun with it. You'll be getting another note tomorrow and that will give you further details. I think this is really clever," William said.

"I don't see anything **clever** at all," Nigel shouted as he crossed his arms in front of his belly.

"Nigel," Abigail said sweetly. "Someone obviously likes you or they wouldn't have played this prank on you. They know that you're always joking around and that you love to tease people. Think of this as a compliment. You have to know that everyone here loves you."

Nigel pouted for a little while longer. He finally looked at Abigail and smiled. "I guess you're right, Abigail. I'm good at handing it out, so I've got to take it when the joke's on me."

"There you go," William said. "Now let's put our heads together and see if we can beat the Horse Whisperer at his own game. Give me a step-by-step rundown of what you did with FANCY DANCY."

"Okay. I went out on the patio and painted my horse all black. I want to dress him up in spats and a tux, so I thought a large, red bow tie would look good."

"Spats and a bow tie?" William asked.

"Yeah—like Fred Astaire used to wear. I had some old, black plastic plates that I used to make spats. They really look good. Well, anyway, I decided to go to The Yard Goods Store to get material to make a bowtie."

"Nigel, sometime we ought to have a brain surgeon examine your head. It seems to work in strange ways," William teased.

"The lady at the store was very nice. In fact she made me a bow tie and it looks great. Now all we have to do is find my horse," Nigel insisted.

"Let me ask you this…do you think the paint was dry when the crime was committed?" William asked, using a serious tone.

"It wasn't when I left. I was gone about two hours since I did some other errands," Nigel related.

"Well, we might be able to find the thief by checking hands. The thief had to touch the horse somewhere to lift him up and take him away. That means someone could have unexplained black paint on their hands. Now, we must find a way to check out our suspects."

"Oh, how clever of you, William," Abigail said proudly. "See, Nigel, this is going to be fun."

"Tonight, in the dining room, you and I can casually talk with people and, well, let's say, we reach out to shake their hands. We can spot if anyone has black streaks on his hands. You can do this, Nigel. You love to talk and people like to talk with you. You may find the thief right under your nose," William said as Abigail nodded her head in agreement.

"Wait a minute. William, are you trying to tell me that you took FANCY DANCY?"

"What am I going to do with you? I did **not** take your horse." Exasperated, William said, "Someone might have been walking by your patio and saw you working on the horse. Do you remember seeing anyone?" William asked, trying not to lose his patience with his friend.

Nigel put his hand under his chin. "No. I probably had my back towards the walkway. But, I'm determined to catch this guy."

"It could be a woman, you know," William reminded Nigel.

"Nah. I doubt that. How about you, Abigail?" Nigel said as he put his hand out.

"Nigel, I'm surprised at you," Abigail teased. "I would never do that," she said as she held out both her hands for Nigel to inspect.

∗∗∗

The dinner crowd was slowly filling most of the tables. William and Nigel didn't have any problems getting people to talk with them since word of the kidnapping had obviously spread. Consequently, they were able to shake a lot of hands, but to no avail.

When Ellie May heard of Nigel's dilemma, she hurried to his side. "Nigel, I don't know if you read Arthur Conan Doyle's stories of Sherlock Holmes, but you may want to read his *Silver Blaze.* It's a tale about a stolen horse. Well, any way, it's considered Doyle's display of perfect logical deduction. It may give you some ideas on how to find your horse," Ellie May suggested.

Nigel didn't know how to react. Why would he take time to read a story when he was busy looking for his horse? "Thanks, Ellie May. Maybe I'll do that later," he said, hoping to placate her.

"Didn't see anything yet, William," Nigel said as he took his seat forlornly.

"Don't give up. We'll greet people on our way out." Williams urged.

Just then Celeste walked up to the table and sat down. "Okay if I join you?" Celeste asked as she carefully placed a bandaged-wrapped hand on the table.

Nigel took one look and almost dropped his water glass. "Oh, my dear," he said a bit too eagerly, "what happened to your hand? Did you run over it with your little red wagon?"

"How did you guess? I wasn't watching what I was doing the other day, and I upset a wagon-load of books on my right hand. Of course, it had to be the hand I write with. You should have seen me get dressed tonight. I had one hellava time getting this blouse on. You know, it's damned hard to button a blouse with one hand."

Nigel shook his head. "Gee, that's too bad, Celeste. One can hurt their hands in a variety of ways, you know?"

"What? What does that mean, Nigel?" Celeste asked trying to get the gist of Nigel's remark.

"Well, for instance, one could get hurt during the commission of a crime," Nigel said as he pursed his lips.

Celeste wrinkled her brows together. "Nigel, I know you're peculiar at times, but you lost me on this one. Are you suggesting that I committed a crime? If you keep this up, I just might and, be warned, it would definitely be murder."

"Celeste, please forgive Nigel. His horse was kidnapped today, and he's beside himself with worry. He assumed that you might be the one because the thief would have black paint on his hands since the horse was out on the patio to dry when he was taken. And, when he spied the bandage, he thought he had found the rascal," William tried to explain.

Celeste doubled up with laughter. "Maybe he ran away. You should have closed the damned barn door. Nigel, you're something else. What would we ever do here without you?"

Nigel turned red. "Go ahead. Make fun of me. But you can't blame me. I want my horse back," he said just like a child who had lost a tricycle.

"He's supposed to get a ransom note tomorrow, Celeste. We may find out where the horse is then," Abigail explained sweetly.

"I'm getting a little suspicious of that new guy…you know…that Ben fellow," Nigel said.

"What? Just a minute ago it was Celeste," William argued.

"I was wrong. But think about it…we don't know much about him and he does have bushy eyebrows," Nigel argued.

"What do bushy eyebrows have to do with this?" William asked.

"He looks like a thief," Nigel stated.

"Nigel, you need to stop this foolishness. Wait till you get the note tomorrow and maybe your problem will be solved," Celeste argued. "Don't you think that's the sensible way?"

Nigel pouted for a few minutes. Then he sat up straight and said, "Okay. I'll take that advice. But, if the thief hurts one hair on my horse's head, there will be hell to pay."

"Nigel, he's a wooden horse. He doesn't have hair on his head," William drawled.

"You can't see his hair, but I can. He's real to me," Nigel said as he stomped off.

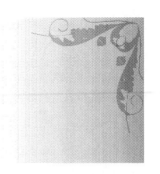

CHAPTER 30

Nigel was having a restless night. He kept waking up and looking out on the patio for the ransom note. He also was hoping to see the kidnapper in person. In the morning, when he brushed his teeth, he took a look at himself in the mirror and admitted that he looked terrible. His eyes were bloodshot. No wonder—this Horse Whisperer had to be a cruel person. He just couldn't think of a person here at MGH who would be that despicable—except for the new guy, Ben.

As he sat at his kitchen table, aimlessly stirring his coffee, he suddenly spied a white envelope on the living room floor. He jumped up. Someone must have shoved it under the front door. He whipped the door open, certain he was going to catch the criminal. To his dismay, the hallway was empty.

He hurried over to his chair and sat down. His hands were shaking as he tore at the envelope.

> *FANCY DANCY is doing just fine—for now.*
> *However, if you do not deliver five pounds of*
> *Toby's Peanut Butter Melts to the front desk by*
> *1 p.m., I will be busy making saw dust. Make*

sure the candy is wrapped in plain white paper
and is placed on the front desk with orders for
no one to touch it. If I see you in The Square, you
can forget the spats and the bow tie—you won't
need them for sawdust.

Have a nice day.
Yours truly,
The Horse Whisperer

Still in his pajamas, Nigel ran to William's apartment and banged on the door.

As William opened the door, he said, "My God, Nigel, you scared the hell out of me. What's wrong now?"

"Here, read this," he said as he pushed the note in front of his friend's face.

William started to chuckle. "Oh, this is funny," he said.

"William, how come, when I have a problem it's funny? When you have a problem, the world has to stop. Now tell me, what's the difference?" Nigel asked, obviously upset.

"Go get the chocolates. Do as the note says. Put the box on the front desk and go away."

"Go away…go away…how will I find the thief that way? And, how do I know he'll return my horse? Now tell me that, buddy," an agitated Nigel spit out.

"Listen, do as I said. I'll fill in for you in *The Square* and I'll keep an eye open for the thief. That should work," William said, trying to convince Nigel.

"I guess you're right. I'll do as the note instructs. But don't you fail me. I want to know who that cockamamie thief is," Nigel ordered as he stomped off to his apartment. "And, if it is that bushy browed Ben, I'll run him out of here."

Before too long, a white-papered, wrapped box was sitting on the front desk. Mary Beth had received instructions to just let the box sit there and the owner would be picking it up. Her interest was definitely piqued, but she was so busy with handling a ladies group that was touring the facilities that she quickly forgot all about it.

William was wandering around, trying not to look out of place with all the women gadding about. It seemed that the women were everywhere. They discovered Hannah's Meditation Room and were enthralled with its décor. They visited the Tech room and were amazed at what they discovered. William had found it necessary—several times—to step out of their way as they excitedly shared what they found with one another. After the confusion, when he looked back at the desk, the package was gone.

William was panicky. He scurried around, trying to see if he could spot someone carrying the white box. All he saw were fancy hats and large purses. He realized that the box could be in one of those handbags. How was he going to explain this to Nigel?

Just then a woman tapped him on the shoulder, "Excuse me, sir. You look vaguely familiar. Did you ever play in a country western band?"

Taken by surprise, William said slowly, "Why...yes...I did. That was a long time ago, though."

"I used to go to Thompson Town all the time to the dances they held at the fire company. I think that's where I saw you," she said.

"M'am, you have a good memory. I'm impressed."

"In fact, I had a secret crush on you then," she said as she blushed.

"Oh, there you are Hilda. We're ready to go," one of her friends said.

The woman thanked him for his time, waved her handkerchief at him and sauntered away with her friend.

Walking down the hall, William was still smiling about Hilda's remarks, but he quickly came back to his senses when he realized that he still had to tell Nigel that he came up empty-handed on the identity of the thief. He had to tuck away his brief encounter with fame. Hesitantly, he knocked on Nigel's front door.

"Come in," Nigel responded.

When William opened the door, there was Nigel sitting on the floor with FANCY DANCY by his side, dressed up in spats and a bow tie.

Nigel was all smiles. "Look who came home" Nigel said proudly.

William sank down to the floor, put his head in his hands and shook his head.

"I found him out on the patio just ten minutes ago. He's fine. He's in good health."

"Nigel, Nigel, he's a wooden horse. Oh, what the hell. If you want him to be real, then he's real."

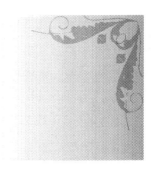

CHAPTER 31

It was Derby Day at Morning Glory Hill and it was a glorious day. Racing fans were arriving early so they wouldn't miss anything and they were looking forward to *Meet and Greet the Horses* that would begin at one. Meanwhile, a van from Yocum's Bar Service had just pulled into the driveway with all the equipment necessary to serve mint julips. Rebecca's crew was preparing to serve hamburgers and hot dogs. Preston and his crew were putting the finishing touches on the platform that would be used to display the horses for the beauty contest. Another van, hauling a load of folding chairs, was backing into the area near the racecourse that had already been laid out in white chalk. There seemed to be workers everywhere.

"Preston, will you please bring a small table out here to hold the dice cage until Barry starts the race," Hortense said. After she walked around a bit, she said, "It looks like everything is under control. Oh, don't forget to put chairs where you have the sellers' tables. And, before I forget, Harvey will be bringing a tote board that he created to let the bettors know how much is being bet on each horse and what the current odds are. He wrote some kind of program that will spit out the information in no time at all. As far as I'm concerned, I think these computers are just way too smart and way too intrusive," she said as she went back into the building.

Promptly at one, the owners starting arriving with their horses in tow. It certainly was a strange sight—bright colors, plumes and feathers, and lots of plastic jewelry. As the proud owners placed their horses on the platform in front of the correct post position number, Barry picked up the mic. "Welcome racing fans to *Meet and Greet the Horses*. Each owner has two minutes to tell you something about the horse he/she is entering in the race. We'll begin with horse number one, LOVELY ABIGAIL."

"Folks, I have to admit that LOVELY ABIGAIL is the class of the race. She has beaten every horse that she has raced against. Owners tremble when they know they have to race against this brilliant filly. If you want a winner, then LOVELY ABIGAIL is what you're looking for." William jested as he gave his horse a gentle pat on the rump.

"Now, horse Number Two, BIG BAD BEN," Barry announced.

"BIG BAD BEN lives up to his awesome name. He has raced with the best in Dubai and beat all those high-priced horses owned by the sheiks. Even his muscles have muscles. His super long legs will get him over the finish line first. Look at his form—a definite winner," Ben said proudly.

"Number Three, FANCY DANCY," Barry said as he handed the mic to Nigel.

"Now hear this, folks. Someone was so afraid of my horse that they held him for ransom. His ability is as great as his namesake—Fred Astaire, and he looks more handsome than any of the other horses," Nigel crowed.

"Now, owned by our only female, Number Four, RAVISHING ROSIE."

"RAVISHING ROSIE not only looks beautiful, she's one of SECRETARAT'S offspring, a Triple Crown Winner. Talk about class! Look at those fishnet stockings, those high heels, and, oh, those gold earrings. She practically flies down the track as light as the wind. Bet on Number Four and you will be a winner," Rosebud said as she blew a kiss to the crowd.

"Now we have a shipper from Nassau, Number Five, BAHAMA MAMA."

"BAHAMA MAMA is from the islands. The other owners know that she's dynamite on the track. Nothing stops her. No matter what these other horses may wear, it doesn't bother her. When she's on the track, all she wants to do is to win. Number Five will earn you money," Gordon said happily.

"Our last entry, Number Six, PRETTY AS A PICTURE." Barry said.

"Folks, now that you have heard the trash talk, I'll let you in on a secret. PRETTY AS A PICUTRE has the form and ability of a sure winner. Look at her. Her body reflects that of a true race horse. She does one thing when she's on the track--WINS!" Harry professed.

The crowd was going bonkers. They cheered each horse and applauded wildly. Everyone was having a great time, not only with the horses, but with the mint julips. Once again, the ladies were wearing hats—replicating what they had seen when they had watched the Kentucky Derby the previous week.

A slight breeze was blowing. A picture perfect day for the derby. It was a festive sight with colorful pennants lined up along the racecourse. Not everyone, however, was interested in the event. Samuel and Julia were not in sight. Enid had looked around for her sister, hoping that she would relent and have some fun with the other residents. Enid decided that she would walk over to her sister's apartment to see if she could coax her out of her apartment. After knocking on the door twice, Enid turned away. In the past, no matter what she had tried, she simply could not find a way to really become friends with her own sister. Well, maybe later. Maybe Nigel might have an idea. He was always so clever.

Barry Adams picked up the mic and said, "Tickets for the derby are now on sale. They are ten dollars each. Remember, folks, one-half of what is bet on the Derby will go to the food bank. Frank and Celeste are ready to sell... sell...sell. Oh, don't forget the mint julips. I've heard that they can help to clear your mind so that you can pick out the winning horse."

Hortense, Mary Beth and Rebecca began to walk around the platform, where the horses were lined up for the beauty contest. They would point out various features to one another and dutifully make notes on the score sheets. After all, a valuable certificate was at stake here, so they needed to make certain that they didn't overlook anything that these crazy owners had attached to their horses. They scurried off to the side for a conference. Finally, Hortense folded the score sheet and handed it to Barry.

Nigel was beside himself. He wanted that certificate badly, but he realized that somehow FANCY DANCY didn't look as colorful as the other horses. Then he rationalized that it had to be that way since Fred Astaire wasn't colorful, but was elegant, charming, brilliant, and captivating.

Barry cleared his throat. "Ladies and gentlemen, may I have your attention please. The judges have made their final decision regarding the most beautiful entry for the Derby. And...and...the winner is RAVISHING ROSIE!"

Rosebud screamed and ran up to the platform. Grabbing the mic out of Barry's hand, she said, "Thank you so much. ROSIE and I both thank you."

Nigel glared at Rosebud. She was really getting on his nerves. He didn't want to be a good sport, but he had to put on an act so he rushed over to Rosebud and gave her a hug. However, he did whisper in her ear, "I think it was fixed."

Rosebud gave Nigel a nice smile and planted a kiss on his cheek.

After an hour or so of ticket selling, the announcement was made that it was finally time for the Derby. Harvey wheeled out his tote board so the spectators could see what each horse would pay if it won the race. The excitement level rose considerably.

"Quiet, please, folks." When the crowd finally settled down, he said, "In this bird cage, there are three dice all numbered from one to six. There are twenty steps from the beginning of the race to the end. I will shake the cage and let the dice settle down. The numbers on the dice will dictate which horse, or horses, will move one or more steps. For instance, if the dice read 2, 4, and 5 then each of those horses moves one step forward. If they read 3,3, and 1, then the 3 horse moves two steps and the 1 moves one. Questions?

"Okay, jockeys, take your positions alongside your horse. You may only move your horse when I tell you. And, remember, we will not tolerate any swearing, punching or kicking. I must caution you that no weapons are allowed on the track. All guns muse be checked with me," Barry joked. "Jockeys, you must go through an inspection before we allow you on the track."

Stretch came out the door, dressed in his jockey silks and carrying a whip. The crowd was yelling so loudly that Barry was having a hard time being heard. "Quiet, folks. As you can see, nothing will get by this inspector," Barry said as Stretch checked each of the jockeys, poking and prodding, even looking into their ears. When he got to Nigel, he poked his tummy and just shook his head from side to side. When it was Rosebud's turn to be examined, he stepped back, took a long hard look, and whistled. The crowd was thoroughly enjoying this frivolity. Stretch walked over to Barry and whispered in his ear.

"Folks, Stretch has just reported that while he's slightly suspicious of one or two of these jockeys, he will allow the race to go on."

Just about everyone was now standing up, Much to the surprise of everyone, one of William's band members then stepped out the door dressed just like the trumpeter at the race track. The crowd yelled once again. Then the trumpeter played the *Call to Post*. Frank then pulled the trigger on his toy gun and Barry shook the cage for the first leg of the race. The crowd suddenly quieted down.

"The numbers are 1, 4, and 5 so LOVELY ABIGAIL, RAVISHING ROSIE, and BAHAMA MAMA each may move one step forward."

With each shake of the cage, everyone was totally immersed in watching the horses move slowly down the raceway. And, when the number 6 came up three times, the screaming got even louder as PRETYY AS A PICTURE moved three steps. When the horses were nearing the end of the race course, the 3, FANCY DANDY, 4, RAVISHING ROSIE, and the 6, BAHAMA MAMA were almost side by side. Nigel was wishing for a double for his horse, but Rosebud's horse only needed one step to captivate the trophy. Nigel held his breath while Barry shook the cage.

Then Barry announced, "Number 5, BAHAMA MAMA may move one step. Number 4, RAVISHING ROSIE may move 2 steps and goes over the line! I declare that RAVISHING ROSIE wins the Derby!" Barry screamed.

Nigel was crushed but he put on a happy face and shook Rosebud's hand. "Congratulations, Rosebud."

"How gracious of you, Nigel. By the way, Phillip and I certainly enjoyed the peanut butter melts."

CHAPTER 32

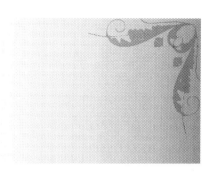

"Look, William, I can still see traces of the chalk lines that were used in the Derby last week. I would have thought that by now the rain would have washed them all away," Abigail said.

"One more good rain and they will completely disappear and the Derby will only be a distant memory. On the other hand, I'm not too sure that Nigel will ever get over losing to Rosebud," William said as he chuckled. "He was trounced," William said as he laughed

"He did give her a kiss on her cheek, though. That was a good sign," Abigail added.

"Talk about the devil and he appears," William said as he spotted Nigel walking up the path leading to the gazebo.

"Hi, you two lovebirds. Do you come out here to bill and coo?" Nigel asked as he puckered up his lips.

Abigail moved over to make room on the bench for Nigel. "Here, Nigel, sit beside me and enjoy this perfect day. William and I find that just spending time out here for thirty minutes or so, seems to make all things brighter."

Nigel heaved a big sigh and managed to squeeze himself in the open space. "When I think of how Rosebud managed to get all that candy out of me I still see red," he huffed and puffed.

"Now, now, Nigel you know that you ate up all that attention. Rosebud truly likes you," William argued.

"The operative word is *likes.* Pardon me if I don't get all warm and fuzzy over that," Nigel said in a grumpy tone.

"Look on the bright side. We raised over four thousand dollars for the food bank. That will really help them out. Come on, now, Nigel, you knew for a long time that Rosebud was only a friend. And, you have to admit, she's always been a good one," William rationalized.

Nigel was quiet for a few minutes. "Yeah, you're right. I just hated to lose the Derby to her since I know that Phillip had a hand in kidnaping my horse. Well, that's over. Now, what's next?" Nigel asked hopefully.

"A big wedding is coming up soon," Abigail reminded them. "And, don't forget, the Harvest Moon Bazaar isn't too far away."

Nigel thought a minute, and then he said, "You know, I think what I need is some good luck. I want to turn things around in my life. Or, should I visit a fortune teller to see if anything exciting is planned for my future? Well, what do you suggest?" Nigel asked.

"Luck will find you," Abigail said.

"You've got to be kidding. Luck couldn't find me with a high-beam torch," Nigel said despondently.

"I know a few traditions that people use to increase their luck,." William said. "But, they seem to work only on New Years' Eve/"

"Why can't I use them now? After all, I don't want to wait that long," Nigel argued.

"Well, I had a friend who would put silver coins on the windowsill of the window nearest his front doorway. He always used shiny half-dollars—claimed that it worked. However, in my family we would eat pork and sauerkraut on the first day of January. Can't say that I ever saw any difference in what happened in my life but my mom wouldn't think of making anything else on that day," William explained.

"Those ideas sound crazy," Nigel said.

"Oh, and going to a fortune teller sounds better?" William challenged. "Just relax, Nigel. By the way you seem to be paying a great deal of attention to Enid. How's that going?" William inquired. "Maybe that's all the good luck you need, old boy."

"Look, William, don't go drawing any conclusions. Enid and I are good friends. After all, with the kind of sister she has she needs someone who's nice to her," Nigel said. "She's working with Harry and Harvey in creating an exhibit for the Harvest Moon Bazaar. It has something to do with her teapot collection. Harvey thinks she can win first place. Wouldn't that frost her sister?" Nigel said as he giggled.

"Nigel, are you still planning on doing something for the Harvest Moon Bazaar?" Abigail asked.

"I was thinking of giving dancing lessons. You know, I could set up a small dance floor and give a thirty minute lesson. What should I charge for that? Remember, it's for charity."

"I think at least twenty-five," Abigail suggested. "I think the ladies would really like that, Nigel."

"Oh, there goes Samuel," William said as he pointed to a passing car. "Look, look, Julia's by his side. This place is getting to be like Peyton Place—remember that sexy book they turned into a racy TV series? Everyone in the town had some kind of secret they were hiding. By the way, Nigel, you once said that you felt that Samuel was hiding a dark secret. Remember, you even said that if it was true that I would owe you a round-trip ticket of Las Vegas. And, if you don't find out anything about Samuel you will hear me reminding you about it forever."

"That bet is still on," Nigel said assuredly. "I know he's up to something. I've seen some strange goings and comings involving him. I'll catch him yet. And when I do, I'll rub his nose in it." Nigel stood up and made a fist.

"Nigel, I'm surprised at you. How can someone so utterly handsome be so mean?" Abigail asked.

Nigel blushed. He stuttered a bit, shoved his hands into his pockets, and quietly left the gazebo.

"Oh," Abigail said, "I didn't mean to hurt his feelings."

"Don't worry, Abigail, Nigel will always be Nigel. In no time at all, he'll have forgotten what you said. You, my dear, shouldn't spend one moment worrying about that," William said as he slipped his arm around Abigail's shoulders.

Just then, Nigel turned around and came running back. Huffing and puffing, he said, "Abigail, I promise I won't do anything nasty to Samuel. But, I will discover his secret." Then he spun around and hurried away.

CHAPTER 33

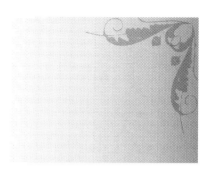

"Remember the first time we came to *Marie's Closet*?" Marty asked Ellie May and Rosebud. "We were getting ready for our prom. Now, here we are, shopping for my wedding dress," Marty said as she began looking through the rack of short formal dresses.

"That's when Marie Turnbull was the owner. I'm glad to see that the shop hasn't lost its charm. Is Marie coming, Marty?" Rosebud asked.

"Oh my, yes. I don't want to choose something that she doesn't like," Marty said.

"It's your wedding. Just because she's your wedding planner doesn't mean that you must do everything she says," Rosebud said a bit testy.

"She also wants to see Julia, the new owner," Marty said hoping that if she ignored the sharpness of her tone, Rosebud might relax.

"Oh no, not another Julia?" Ellie May said apprehensively.

Marty laughed. "Julia Eckenroth is a gracious lady. She has an adorable New York accent and is well-known for her own designs. Here she comes now."

"Ladies, this is an exciting day for you. Getting ready is half the fun of a wedding. Marie called me yesterday and told me that she would be dropping by, and I'm anxious to see her again," Julia said warmly. "Now, our beautiful bride-to-be, what are you looking for?"

"Short. I don't want a long gown. Maybe a two-piece dress or a suit. Or, perhaps even ankle-length. I'm turning myself over to you. I have my advisors with me and of course I want to please them. Frank's daughters will be here too, but they said they want to give me time to make my decision first. Isn't that thoughtful of them?" Marty said excitedly.

"Let's move to the next room. I have some fetching things to show you, Marty. Are you leaning towards a specific color?" Julia asked as she led the way.

"I was thinking silver, light pink, gray—gee, I'm just not sure."

"Here's one of my originals. It's a faille fabric, but feel how soft it is. I also have this in a soft silver silk," Julia said as she pulled another dress from the rack. "I think you'll be happier with ankle-length, since it helps to create a more formal look. How about sleeves? Yes or no?"

"Yes, I need sleeves. I'm much too old to have my arms bare," Marty said.

"Marty, are you sure you don't want a floor-length gown?" Rosebud asked hopefully.

"That's the one thing I'm certain of. Julia, let's begin with these two and then we can go from there," Marty suggested.

Just then Marie came into the store. She hurried over to Julia and the two women greeted one another warmly.

"Wow! Marty that looks terrific!" Marie said as she watched Marty twirl around.

Ellie May and Rosebud were both looking through the racks of dresses. They each picked out one dress and Marty agreed to try them both.

After trying on the tenth dress, Marty finally said, "I still like the silver silk dress best."

"Alright, then, try that one on again, just to be certain," Julia recommended.

By the time Frank's daughters arrived, Marty had not only settled on her dress, but she had also chosen a small ornament for her hair. As she walked back and forth in front of the tri-fold of mirrors, Marty could not help but smile. Here she was, a senior citizen, getting ready for a wedding to someone who had simply walked into her life when he had invited her to attend a prom at Morning Glory Hill. As soon as she spotted *her girls,* she rushed to their side.

"Well, what do you think?" Marty asked as she turned around. "Do you think your dad will like this?"

"Marty, you could wear a barrel with straps and he would think you looked spectacular," Cora said.

"Beautiful, simply beautiful," the other three sisters simultaneously agreed.

"Ladies, let's start pulling things off the rack for you to try on. If you would like, we could use one of you as a model while the others keep looking around. You all look like you wear the same size," Julia said.

"I'm the hippy one," Lucy confessed. "Keep that in mind."

Marie sat beside Marty as they watched the parade of women and clothes going to and from the dressing rooms. "Marty, I think it's wonderful that Frank's daughters have taken to you in such a warm manner."

"I'm a lucky woman. I never expected to get married again, let alone to a man who is bringing with him four wonderful girls. I can't tell you how I worried about the whole thing—you know—whether or not they would accept me. Little did I know that that would be the least of my worries, but wait, I don't have any worries," Marty said as she laughed.

"You're going to have one big wedding party," Marie said. I know Gretchen will probably be your flower girl. But who will be Frank's best man?"

"He's chosen his oldest son-in-law. It was a tough decision for him but his girls helped him to narrow his choices down," Marty explained.

When Ellie May came out of the dressing room with a pale pink ankle-length dress with a draped bodice and a little crocheted jacket, Marty almost cried. "I love that," she said quietly.

Julia immediately went to Rosebud with the same dress. "Marty wants you to try this on."

Rosebud was over her snit. When she stepped out of the dressing room, and stood alongside of Ellie May, the two bridesmaids joined hands and smiled at Marty. "I have one request, Marty, must I be a matron of honor? It sounds so old."

Marie was anxiously waiting to see what Julia had chosen for Frank's daughters. She was thrilled that the women were anxious to be part of the wedding. When the four of them walked into the front room of the shop, Marty said, "Yes, oh my yes. Ladies you look stunning."

"While their dresses are very similar in design, they are a shade darker than the matrons of honors' gowns. Marie, what's your opinion?"

"You nailed it, Julia."

Marty stood up. "Ladies, after all this hard work, it's time to party. Next stop, *Ryan's Bar and Grill.*"

CHAPTER 34

Ben was restless. He had been able to immerse himself in a book about Alexander Hamilton but when his back began to ache, he got up and walked around the living room. As he looked at the clock and saw that it was a little after one a.m. he decided to walk to *The Night Owl*. Being one of the newest residents at MGH he wanted to learn all he could about this place that his wife and he now call *home*. Tossing his checkered bathrobe robe over his bright red pajamas, he hurried out the door and down the hallway, or maybe he should think of it as a lane.

As he cut across *The Square*, he saw that there were people seated at the front table. Hoping that he would know whoever was there, Ben was relieved when he spotted William and Nigel. While he knew that William was a friendly person, he wasn't too sure about Nigel.

"Hello, gentlemen. Mind if I join you?" Ben asked.

"Always room for one more," William said as he pulled out a chair for the newcomer.

Nigel looked up. There were those bushy eyebrows he disliked so much. "Hello," Nigel said in a noncommittal manner.

"How did you enjoy our little Derby?" William asked.

"It was so much fun. Nigel, your horse looked spectacular. I loved that you put spats on him. I thought that bow tie was great too. You sure have an incredulous imagination. Trixie, tells me that she has heard you're one hellava dancer. It must be great to have so much talent," Ben said.

Nigel was now looking at Ben in a different light. Apparently the man knew good taste when he saw it. He had to give him credit for that. "I understand that your wife is an author—children's books I heard," Nigel said.

"Yes. In fact one year she won an award for the outstanding children's book. My Trixie is well known among school librarians," Ben said proudly.

"Ah, Trixie, I love that name. You remember there was a Trixie on the Jackie Gleason Show—the upstairs neighbor, I think," Nigel said in a friendly tone.

"Oh what laughs we used to get from that show. What was it Gleason used to say to his wife? *To the moon Alice.* Was that it?" William asked.

"You know, we just don't have comedy shows like that anymore. I can't stand those stupid housewife shows—you know, where the women parade around half naked and all they do is fight with one another," Ben said.

"I don't mind the half-naked, but I can't stand the shrieking and bawling over who said what when," Nigel said as they all laughed. "Wait a minute, I just got a great idea! Wouldn't it be funny if we could produce an MGH housewives show? If we get the ladies to wear satin dresses two sizes too small, and cut down to the belly button, and have them wear six-inch heels, we might have an award-winning show. People will come from miles around just to see it!"

"Yeah, that would be the day," William said. "I don't mean to throw cold water on your idea but that will never happen."

"Who says?" Nigel snapped.

"Okay, guys," Jake said. "I hate to interrupt your argument, but as manager of this fine establishment, I want recommended the chocolate cake tonight or the banana pudding pie. Which do you prefer?"

After hearing three chocolate cake orders Jake asked, "With ice cream?"

"Do chickens have lips?" Nigel asked as Jake went back into the kitchen.

"Nigel, again I ask you. What the hell does that mean? You say that a lot but I still don't know what it means."

"If one must ask what that means, then one missed the point all together," Nigel said facetiously. "You need to develop a finely-honed sense of humor like I have."

William rolled his eyes.

"I was glad to see you guys here. It's one a.m. and I wasn't sure there would be anyone here. As a matter of fact, I have something that I would like to run by you fellows," Ben said. "The other night I got home from a trip to Philadelphia around two in the morning. When I pulled into my parking space in the garage, I saw a light coming from underneath the door of the storage area. And, I even thought I had heard music. But, I was too tired to go over there to check it out. Later, when I had given it some thought, I realized

I should have investigated a bit—but then again—burglars wouldn't play music."

Nigel sat up straight. His mind went directly to Samuel. "What kind of music?" Nigel asked.

"I don't remember but it was peppy—you know—the kind you could dance to. That's all I remember. It's too late now. I hope it wasn't some vagrant taking up residence or some teenagers getting into trouble. I guess I'll pass that on to Hortense some time," Ben said.

While the trio moved on to talk about other things, Nigel's mind was still on Samuel. He remembered the time that he had seen Samuel and Julia carrying overnight bags and walking through the garage. All of this fits—just like a jigsaw puzzle. Without clueing in anyone else, Nigel began to make a plan. He would begin by investigating the storage area himself. Watch out Samuel, I'm coming for you.

CHAPTER 35

Marty had given strict orders to Ellie May and Rosebud that there would be no bridal shower. At first, her friends had been crushed. So, they decided to "end run" her by honoring the occasion with a luncheon. The party invitations indicated that while the celebration would be for Marty, no presents would be allowed. However, if guests wanted to donate goods or money to the Food Bank, they could do so.

Miracles of all miracles, they had been able to keep Marty in the dark. It was difficult for Ellie May and Rosebud to keep a secret about any of the arrangements. The two were standing outside her door, while they kept checking their watches.

Ellie May leaned close to Rosebud and whispered, "Preston is due any minute, but we need to wait until we're sure he's ready to play his part. We need to keep her away from *Sassy's* and get her to the dining room. So he's going to give her some excuse so she won't be too suspicious that we aren't going *to Sassy's* as we usually do for lunch. Oops, there he is now." She waved to Preston and he stepped back. "Okay, Rosebud, ring the bell."

When her doorbell rang, Marty shouted, "Come in."

"Are you ready to go to lunch?" Ellie May asked.

"Sure am," she said as she looked askance at her friends. "Are you two up to something?"

"No, and it's all your fault. You said you didn't want a bridal shower. I guess you know you spoiled our fun," Rosebud said dejectedly.

As Marty was about to lock her door, Preston appeared with his toolbox in hand. "Are you on your way to *Sassies* for lunch? They're closed due to a water pipe break, but the dining room's open. Marty, is it okay if I fix your dishwasher while you're gone?"

"I didn't know anything was wrong with it," Marty said.

"Well, I finally got that rubber gasket it needs around the door. Sometimes it takes forever to get these parts," Preston explained.

"Sure, go ahead and thank you, Preston," Marty said.

"I'll lock up when I go," Preston said as he closed the door behind him.

"Marty, how does it make you feel when you think about not only getting a new husband, but also four grown daughters and all those grandchildren and even great grandchildren?" Ellie May asked as they walked across *The Square.*

"Lucky. Very lucky. My son's also looking forward to having sisters," Marty mentioned. "He told me the other day that it was going to be hard for him to share me with them—wasn't that sweet? Look, the dining room entrance door is closed. I wonder if they're really open," Marty stated.

Rosebud quickly pulled the door open. When all sixty guests shouted "Surprise!" Marty jumped.

"Girls," Marty whispered, "I thought I..."

"This is not a bridal shower. This is a party honoring you but giving all the gifts to the Food Bank," Rosebud explained as she waved her arms towards the stage.

Marty was astounded. There were stacks and stacks of canned goods on several tables. Cornucopias of fresh vegetables were lined up around the tables as if they were guarding the food. And, in the center of all of this, was a small pine tree that had money tied to its branches. Marty was speechless.

Rosebud took Marty's hand and led her to the main table. "Marty, sit down before you fall down," she said as she laughed. "I'm so pleased that we surprised you."

Marty began to cry when she saw that her son was sitting at her table with two of Frank's daughters on one side and the other two women on the other side. "Oh. Oh," was all she could manage.

After a luncheon was served, the curtains on the stage opened. When the guests spied William at the piano with several members of his band around him, they applauded wildly. The trumpeter stood up and played the *call to post*. Nigel, wearing a tuxedo, appeared and the crowd applauded once again. He bowed to Marty, extended his hand, and led her to the center of the dance floor. As the first strains of *I Could Have Danced All Night* were played, Nigel took Marty in his arms and, to the crowd's delight, they waltzed across the floor.

When the featured couple had finished their dance, Barry Adams took the mic and said, "And now, by popular demand, we have another very special guest for you, Marty. You just might know this fellow," he teased as Frank walked through the doorway.

Marty's breath was taken away. As Frank walked toward her, his daughters stood up and applauded. Frank took her in his arms. "Marty, I cannot waltz like Nigel I cannot play the piano like William, but I promise to love you as long as we both live."

Just like youngsters who had found their first love, Frank and Marty were now oblivious to everyone else. He held her close. She put her head on his shoulder—no words were needed—they knew, that for some reason, they were meant to be together and all was right with *their* world. As Marty lifted her head and they kissed, Harry was right there snapping pictures.

CHAPTER 36

Nigel checked the clock—quarter after two. He felt it was time—time to go to the storage room and look around. As he waited for the elevator to take him down to the basement, Nigel kept looking up and down the lane. He wanted to be alone. When the doors opened, he scurried in and quickly pressed the button marked G.

He had never noticed before that the elevator was so noisy. When he stepped off, and the doors closed behind him, everything suddenly was still. He glanced around, making certain that no one else was there. Holding his flashlight by his side, he moved down the hallway and shortly was standing in front of the storage room. William would laugh at him now since Nigel's heart was beating rapidly—why he couldn't be certain.

When he reached the storage room, he saw that there was a sign on the door. Lifting his flashlight, he studied what it said—*No items shall be removed from this room without the expressed consent of Hortense Ferndale or Dr. Samuel Long.*

As he put his hand on the doorknob, he scolded himself for shaking so much. The door opened almost silently. He ran his hand along the wall and quickly found the light switch. He had to blink his eyes several times to figure out what he was really seeing. When he steadied himself, he realized that these were three long mirrors positioned side by side along one wall. Four overhead lights reflected from one mirror to another, casting a dazzling brightness from one end of the room to the other. He remembered a conversation he had with Enid when she told him that she had three floor length mirrors placed in the storage room. Nigel instinctively knew that the mirrors had not been stored in this manner. They had been moved and placed in this position for a specific purpose—but why?.

An unpainted chair was in the center of all the brightness. Something was on the chair. He moved about until he discovered that it was a *Raggedy Ann* doll. Lying on the floor was a plastic rod. He walked over and picked it up. The rod was about two feet long, and what looked like a large powder puff was taped to one end.

There were other boxes and various pieces of furniture stacked on the other side of the room. Nigel stood there for a few minutes studying the scene. Suddenly, he began putting the pieces together. He put his hands on his hips and said, "Samuel you old rat bastard. You think you're clever, but I'm right on your tail!"

CHAPTER 37

It was the day of the wedding. It seemed as though everyone had a place to go and things to do. Traffic in *The Square* had never been so busy. Ladies were hurrying to the beauty shop where every drier was tied up, while hand-held driers were also buzzing away. The doorway to the dining room was closed and yellow tape went from one side to the other. Harvey wanted to be certain that no one could peak in ahead of the appointed time. Late last night, he and the electricians had hung netting over the dance floor area. Harvey loved the idea of having little white lights interspersed in the netting for he knew that, when it was time for dancing, he could turn the lights down low and it would appear as if the dancers were outside enjoying the star-filled sky—he would be certain that when this happened he would have Harry by his side.

The scene inside the dining room was quite similar to the activity in *The Square*. Preston and his crew were using flatbeds to bring in additional tables and chairs from the convention center. Harvey was the commander in chief as he made certain that each table was positioned exactly where he wanted. When he was satisfied, he motioned for the servers to begin dressing the tables. As they opened the special linens that Harvey had personally selected, the ambiance became a sea of gray interwoven with silver. All the while, Hunter Schmidt, videographer from *Brides Today* had his camera perched on his shoulder and was trailing after the crew.

Rebecca came into the room pushing a cart loaded with glassware. Harvey rushed to her side. "Rebecca, that's too heavy for you," he said.

"Ah, come on now, Harvey. I've done this hundreds of times. Remember, I was in the service. Who do you think pushed the carts then?" she teased. "You need to check out the kitchen. Stretch and I have been baking and cooking desserts since early morning. We've got brownies, miniature eclairs, pies, cakes, cookies—and your favorite, Harvey, crème Brule."

"Excuse me, Rebecca, shall we begin to set the tables?" Lucinda asked as she stood among a cadre of servers.

"That's Harvey's domain today. And, be careful. He can be a terror."

"Come on, Rebecca, you know I'm a pussycat," Harvey said as he winked his eye.

As the staff moved from table to table, folding the napkins and placing the champagne and water glasses, Harvey kept a close watch on what they were doing. When they started with the silverware, he quickly called them aside and gave them very specific instructions on how he wanted each utensil placed. He didn't fail to notice that some of them rolled their eyes, but to Harvey, that just meant that he was doing his job.

"Lucinda, on that cart over there are little wicker baskets filled with souvenir pens and notepads. Please put one on each table. These are for guests to write their personal congratulations for the bridal couple," Harvey instructed.

"I was wondering what that fancy little box was for on the table by the doorway. Is that where the notes should be placed?" Lucinda asked. "What a neat-o idea."

"When you have done that, take a break and I'll let you know if there is anything else that must be done. Thank you very much." Harvey then busied himself in the kitchen, helping out where he could, until the florist arrived. Then he was off with the speed of a gazelle.

Marie came rushing in, clipboard in hand, and headed for the delivery men. "Just a minute. Some of those boxes must be taken elsewhere."

"Well, I have one marked for Lilac Lane and another marked for Orchid Lane. I'll need help in finding these places," the delivery man said.

"No problem. I'll go with you. How are things going in here, Harvey?" Marie asked.

"So far, so good. Oops, here comes that photographer again," Harvey said as Harry snapped a few pictures.

"I'll go along, too," Harry said. "I want some shots of both families as they're getting ready. What about you, Hunter?"

Hunter, taking his camera off his shoulder, said, "I'm not interested in the actual wedding. Our video will be for event planners to learn how Harvey was able to create a wedding venue out of such a cavernous space."

"Okay, now where were we?" Harvey said to the other delivery man. "Oh, I want the green vines, interspersed with these white orchids, hanging down the front of the head table. Every table gets a water-filled bowl, placed on a small pedestal. Small bunches of morning glories will float on the water. I want them to look as if they bloomed in that exact place, so please make certain that they hang over the sides of the bowl. I see you have the shrubs I ordered over there. Place them where I have indicated on the diagrams I gave you."

"Harvey, where do you want these tall vases of calla lilies?" the florist asked.

Harvey walked over to a space directly in front of the head table. He paced off two steps and said, "Right here Roger. Put one here where I'm standing and the other one six feet over. They'll frame the area where the ceremony will take place."

"You're not having one of those bowers where the bride and groom stand?" Hunter asked in amazement.

"Nope. The bride hates those," Harvey said as he chuckled.

"Okay, now where do you want the blankets of morning glories?" the florist asked.

"Frame the doorway—inside, of course," Harvey directed.

When the florist was finished, Harvey bounded up the steps to the stage to look over the venue that he had created. He glanced at his watch to make certain that he was still on time. The ceremony was set for six, dinner for one hundred sixty guests was scheduled for seven, and dancing at eight—a perfect time for the little lights. Suddenly he realized that something was missing—it was the LED candles. He had wanted to use real candles, but the rules here at MGH forbade open flames.

He hurriedly called Preston. "My God, Preston, where are the LED candles?"

"They just arrived. I'm bringing them over now. We have lots of time, Harvey. Calm down. I don't want you getting a heart attack—we are much too busy to handle that too," Preston said. "Besides, we really don't want the bride and groom to have to step over your dead body!"

CHAPTER 38

A little after four-thirty, the harpist arrived. Preston was there to carry the harp up the stage steps and to make certain that Shelby Gable had everything she needed. William, looking dapper in his tuxedo, came in the side door and hurried over to greet her.

"Shelby, nice to see you again. It's my understanding that you're playing for about forty minutes before the ceremony and then during dinner. Do I have that right?"

"Yes, I usually start playing when I see guests arriving. Sometimes they come really early and I hate to see them just sitting and waiting, so I play I'll probably leave my harp on the stage for a while after dinner since Marty has invited me to stay for the dancing."

"I'll make sure that my guys are careful around your harp. They can sometimes be a bit clumsy. However, since we won't be playing our usual country-western music, they may just behave themselves," William explained. "I understand that you'll also be playing for Abigail."

"I'm looking forward to that. We've had several practice sessions and I think she's fabulous," Shelby replied.

William winked at Shelby. "I think she's fabulous, too. Well, I've got to run. I'm in the wedding procession, so I better get a move on. See you later," he said as he ran out the side door.

Shelby watched as the servers hurried back and forth, doing last minute adjustments here and there. Marie came in the side door with two young men who Shelby later learned were Frank's grandsons. They opened the main doors to the dining room and there was Sally waiting to get in. Shelby adjusted her long white skirt, put her harp against her shoulder and began playing.

Before too long, almost all the seats had been filled. The music, which floated throughout the dining room, had a calming effect on the guests. Exactly at ten of five, Abigail came from the back of the stage and stood near the microphone. When Shelby played the introduction to *Because* a hush came over the room. Abigail didn't disappoint her fans. Her voice echoed throughout the room and set the tone for the arrival of the bride.

Promptly at five, when Shelby strummed the strings on her harp, the door on the right side of the stage opened and Frank and Rob, his son-in-law, entered and walked to where the tall vases of flowers had been placed. To the surprise and delight of the guests, Frank's daughters, one by one, walked down the same path, each one carrying a single calla lily set off with a bow that matched the color of their dresses. With smiles on their faces, they lined up behind their father.

Shelby began playing *Pachelbel's Canon in D* with a flourish. The door on the left side opened and in stepped Ellie May escorted by William. It was hardly noticeable that she was shaking like a leaf. After they reached the front of the room, Rosebud and Nigel walked down the same path. Nigel was beaming—it felt good to have Rosebud at his side again.

When the guests caught sight of Gretchen in her white organdy dress trimmed in tiny pink roses, they were charmed. Her hair had been pulled back in a ponytail tied with a pale pink ribbon. Her shiny patent leather shoes were offset with white anklets trimmed with lace. She carried a little white basket filled with flower petals that she delicately tossed on the floor. As she came down the aisle and spied Frank, she waved her hand and whispered, "Hi my new Pop Pop."

The guests stood up when Marty, in her gray silk ankle-length dress, entered the room on the arm of her proud son Daniel. Frank's eyes were fixated on her. His smile could not have gotten any wider. He could not believe that someone as wonderful as Marty was marrying him. He watched her every move. While he hadn't been nervous before, he was now. A thought flew through his mind: Suppose she would say *no* when the minister asked her that crucial question. When Reverend Diebert came down the steps of the stage and took his place alongside the groom, Frank focused only on Marty.

Shelby stopped playing and sat back in her chair. Not a sound could be heard. Marty and Frank gazed at one another. For a split second, it was only the two of them. They exchanged knowing glances and seemed at peace with everything. Marty had promised herself that she was not going to cry, and so far she had managed. When she handed her flower over to Rosebud, she clasped hands with Frank. He felt her warm hands and relaxed.

When the minister whispered to him that it was time for him to say his vows, Frank was afraid that he wouldn't be able to speak. He took a deep breath, but when he saw Marty wink at him, he found his voice.

"Marty, I'm a humble man. I don't have the words that you deserve. Ever since the night I took you to the MGH prom, I have loved you. I promise you that I will always love you and take care of you. My girls and I welcome you to our family."

By now it was Frank's daughters who were crying.

"My darling Frank. I remember the night of the prom and how we sat in the gazebo under the stars. I, too, fell in love that night. I'm looking forward to becoming part of your extended family. I promise you that I'll love you and care for you as long as I live."

When they heard the words, '*I now pronounce you man and wife*,' they kissed and then turned around to look at their guests. Amid the applause, the newlyweds took a brief walk down the aisle before they turned and went to the head table. It took a few minutes to get everyone seated.

Rob stepped forward and took the microphone. "Ladies and gentlemen, let's have another round of applause for Mr. and Mrs. Frank Snyder." He paused for a minute. "Please stand for the toast. Dad and Mom—that's the first time I was able to call you that. Well, anyway, now my wife and her sisters finally have a Mom. They tried many times to get one—dragging all sorts of ladies, some even unwilling to come along, to the house to meet their dad. Nothing worked. After Dad moved into MGH, we noticed a change in him. My wife immediately declared that there had to be a woman who brought about this sudden transformation. Marty, do you realize that you not only have a husband, but you just received four daughters, three sons-in-law, eight grandchildren, two great grandchildren and over a dozen dogs, cats, and canaries. Now, if all this makes you want to back out—well, it's too late now. Dad and Mom, with all our hearts we congratulate you, and we wish you both health and happiness." Glasses were raised and the guests said, "Here…here."

Rob handed the mic to Rosebud. "My toast will not take long. Marty, Ellie May and I want to congratulate you and Frank. You make a beautiful couple. We want you to know that we'll always love you. I do have a message from Nigel. He wants you to know that when you need a babysitter for your four new daughters, he's willing to provide that service free of charge."

CHAPTER 39

The noise level in the dining room rose considerably as the guests enjoyed their dinner. Rebecca was handling the kitchen in an amazing manner, never getting ruffled no matter what happened. Stretch was overseeing the additional chefs they had hired for the evening. It took over an hour and a half before everyone had been served.

Harvey was pacing back and forth. He was eager to the turn the lights off and watch the reaction of the crowd. Harry was out of his seat more than he was in it. He must have taken hundreds of shots, but Harvey didn't mind. Photography was Harry's passion and Harry was his passion. When the last tray of desserts had been carried back to the kitchen, Harvey jumped up and headed for the microphone.

"Folks, on your tables you'll see some lanterns. These are LED lights, so push the little switch under the lantern and it will light up. I'm going to turn off the overhead lights shortly. When I do, I want you to look up."

There was a lot of guessing as to what was going to happen next. The LED lanterns began to glimmer. When the lights in the netting lit up, the crowd gasped. The room had magically turned into a very romantic setting for dancing.

"Now, Mr. and Mrs. Frank Snyder, the dance floor is all yours. Marty, we want you to know that Frank selected the song," Harvey said.

William waited until Marty and Frank were in the center of the dance floor. He gave the downbeat and his orchestra began playing *A Pretty Girl is like a Melody.* Then the two of them walked back to their table, amid applause.

From then on, the dance floor was a busy place. Nigel was especially in demand and he was having a great time. However, he didn't fail to notice that even though Samuel and Julia had been invited to the wedding, they were no-shows.

When William announced a fifteen minute break for the orchestra, Nigel hurried out the door and headed for the elevator to the garage. When it stopped, he got out and immediately headed for the storage room. His heart skipped a beat when he saw a glimmer of light seeping out of the bottom of the door. He heard music. He touched the handle of the door—it wasn't locked. He steadied himself—not knowing exactly what he would find. Slowly, inch by inch, he created a space big enough for him to view the room. He blinked his eyes. It was nothing like he had imagined. There was Samuel, wearing a woman's red satin dress and a curly blonde wig. Several strands of pearls were wrapped around his neck. He was tottering across the floor on high-heeled shoes. Then he focused on Julia. She had on a short gingham dress with rows and rows of ruffles. While carrying a lollipop in her hands, she was dancing in patent-leather shoes to the tune of *On the Good Ship Lollipop.*

What happened next shook him even more. Samuel took hold of Julia's arm and pulled her across his lap. He pulled her ruffled panties down, and using the little plastic stick that Nigel had seen before, he began spanking her. In two seconds, Nigel had pulled out his cell phone and began clicking his camera as quickly as he could. It was then that Julia spotted Nigel and she screamed. Samuel stood up, and Julia fell to the floor. Nigel boldly pushed the door fully open.

Finally, Samuel said, "So, what can we do for you?"

Nigel knew he finally had the goods on Samuel. He was relishing being in the catbird seat. The thought of publically humiliating the man was delicious. How many times has Samuel humiliated people visously. He could rip him to shreds in front of all the residents. Samuel would never receive the esteem from the MGH community that he had as a mayor and as a professor with a PhD. He could get even with him for all the mean things that he had ever said. For the first time in his life, Nigel had the upper edge. All those names the kids on the playground used to call him were ringing in his ears. One particular bully used to chant, *rub-a-tub-dub, three men in a tub, oh that's not three men, it's just Nigel.* So, to stop the hurt, Nigel became the class clown. He would tell funny jokes and even make fun of himself, then when the kids laughed, it didn't seem to hurt as much. He was short. He was dumpy. Not much to look at all.

But the insults never stopped—not even here at MGH. He could not bring himself to treat others badly. Jessie popped into his mind. While she had died months ago, he remembered how she use to irritate him when she banged her cane on the floor. But he had kept silent. He was never sure that it was because he was not a mean person, or whether he was afraid that she would do something else to annoy him. Samuel's disrespect continued. Had it not been for his dancing talent, Nigel was certain that he could be classified as a loser. But now, he had power that he never had before. Now he knew something about someone that could destroy their self-wroth and perhaps even their career. He could be the one pointing a finger and ridiculing someone. He's the one who could be laughing. WAIT A MINUTE! That would also mean the Julia would be implicated. AND, that meant that Enid would be dragged into this tawdry mess. He couldn't take such a risk. Enid was a lovely woman and Nigel was fond of her. Actually he was quite fond of of her. She was pretty and feminine and kind. She laughed at his jokes. He hadn't realized before just how fond he was of her. And then, there were all those women who had sought him out at the wedding asking for a dance. He had several true friends like William and Frank. He doubted that Samuel had any friends at all.

Suddenly, however, Nigel experienced an epiphany. He no longer had the desire to defame Samuel. Unable to understand what was happening to him, Nigel felt nothing but extreme sorrow. He remembered how his mother used to say that the wise man holds his tongue.

"Why don't you say something?" Samuel sneered.

Julia was huddled up in a ball on the floor, weeping and trying desperately to cover herself.

But Nigel was silent.

"Say something, you dumb ox."

"I tell you what Samuel. I may well be a *dumb ox*, but I'm not a sick one. You're a brilliant man, but somehow, you've managed to make people despise you. Julia, you have allowed yourself to wallow in jealousy for so long that you've lost your soul. You ran away rather than complimenting Enid on her solo—what a piece of work you are."

Nigel stood perfectly still—just starring at the pathetic couple. Finally, the words came spilling out. "I won't say anything to anyone about this—but only on my terms. I'll give you two options—you choose. Option one is that the two of you must stop your insulting behavior towards everyone and this metamorphism must take place immediately. Option two requires that you move to another facility. If you cannot accept one of my options, I'll blast what I saw here all over the place. Now, you two pathetic animals, do you understand me? Oh, and from now on, this room's out of bounds. Samuel, turn in the key you have to this room by tomorrow morning to Hortense."

"This is blackmail," Samuel shouted as he shook his fist at Nigel.

"Yes, sir, it is. Shall I call our resident lawyer, Gordon Turnbull, so he can provide you with legal advice?" Nigel mocked. He paused for a few seconds. "No? I didn't think so. With that, I'll bid you adieu!"

By the time Nigel returned to the dining room, the orchestra had begun to play again. He hurried over to Enid and said, "My dear, may I have the honor of this dance?"

"Nigel, I missed you. I thought you had left for the night and I was disappointed," Enid said. She was a bit shocked at her boldness.

The servers continued to move about with trays of goodies and the open bar was doing a steady business. No one seemed to notice that Marty and Frank had managed to slip out the back door to the limo that was waiting to whisk them away. When the orchestra played *Good Night Ladies* the guests were disappointed but still reveling in the fun that they had had.

All the overhead lights came on. William jumped off the stage and hurried to Abigail. "Abby, honey, would you mind sticking around a little longer? I want to show you something after everyone is gone."

Abigail smiled, took a seat alongside the stage and watched the band pack up their instruments. Finally, everyone was gone. William turned the overhead lights off, set the timer for the lights in the netting, and plugged in his disc player. When Abigail heard the first few notes, she knew it was *Stardust*—her favorite song.

William held Abigail in his arms and said, "Sweetheart, I couldn't dance with you before. Now, I have you all to myself." As Abigail kissed his cheek, the two of them twirled across the dance floor. It was Abigail who noticed Harry and Harvey first—standing in the doorway. She crooked her finger to indicate that they should come in and join them. So, as the little stars twinkled above them and a beautiful melody filled the air, two couples, obviously in love, experienced a feeling of happiness that they would long remember.

CHAPTER 40

Ellie May, holding her little dog, Sophie, was frantically knocking on Rosebud's door. "Rosebud, it's me, Ellie May. I've got news!"

As she opened her door, Rosebud said, "My goodness—what's wrong? Are you okay?"

"Yes, yes, I'm okay," Ellie May said as she entered the apartment. "It's Samuel...he's moving out."

"Samuel? Are you certain?"

"Yes, there's a truck back there and they're loading it up. Samuel's pacing back and forth with Oscar under his arm. I was walking Sophie when I spotted Samuel with that darn cat of his, so I picked her up. I don't trust Samuel so I surely don't trust that fat overbearing cat," an irritated Ellie May said.

"My goodness—first it was Julia who moved out and now Samuel. What on earth is happening?" Rosebud questioned.

"I got it—maybe they're lovers and they're running away together," Ellie May suggested.

"For heaven's sake, Ellie May. Ever since the wedding two weeks ago, you keep trying to pair everyone up. Lovers? Ridiculous," Rosebud clucked.

"Nigel's back there, too."

"What? Why?" Rosebud asked.

"He's sitting on a lawn chair, watching the movers. He offered to help Samuel, but the old grouch just ignored him," Ellie May explained. "I for one am happy that the egotistical professor is leaving."

"Marty's in for some surprises when she gets back from Maui on Friday. Wait until she sees that the apartment next to hers is vacant again. Oh, by the way, we put that little box of personal congratulations from her wedding guests on her coffee table. Hortense thought that it would be a perfect *welcome home* gift for them," Rosebud said.

"I wonder what's going to happen with the Mayors Council. Maybe Ben would be interested in taking over for Samuel. You know what, Rosebud, I have a feeling that this place will never be the same as it was before. Am I crazy, or what?" Ellie May said.

"Things may be different, but that doesn't necessarily mean they'll be bad. Maybe our little trio may not be able to spend as much time together as we did before. After all, Marty now has a husband, but we'll always be friends," Rosebud tried to assure her friend.

"I hope you're right. Now, I'll take Sophie home and then I'll meet you at *Sassy's*."

Rosebud wanted to take a look at the movers before she went to lunch. She was eager to find out why Nigel was there. *That* really aroused her interest. Nigel disliked Samuel, so why would he be offering to help the man move? Well, she thought it was worth it to take a look.

When she spotted Nigel, she couldn't help but smile. He was wearing over-sized sunglasses and holding a notepad and pen in his hands. "Nigel, what in the hell are you doing?" a curious Rosebud asked.

"Oh, just making a few notes," Nigel said pleasantly.

After the movers closed the doors to the truck, Samuel ran across the lawn with Oscar under his arm. He fumbled with his car keys, tossed Oscar into the back seat, and jumped into his car and sped away. Nigel waved goodbye.

When the driver of the moving truck walked past her, Rosebud asked sweetly, "You men have a long haul ahead of you?"

"About a week," the man said. "I'm not allowed to tell you where, if that's what you really want to know."

CHAPTER 41

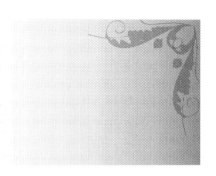

Enid was upset. She had had no idea that her sister was going to move out of MGH. She had to learn that Julia was gone from one of the other residents. She felt guilty. Perhaps she had done something that so offended her sister that she simply took off. For as long as she could remember, Enid felt somehow that she had disappointed Julia. It seemed that no matter what she did or said, Julia would object. Perhaps if she had been a better sister, Julia would still be here. She needed someone to talk with—not Noah. While her son always tried to be helpful, when it came to female issues, he was at a loss. She checked the clock—it would be ten in the morning in Vegas, so her daughter would be wide awake.

On the third ring Helena answered, "Hello, Mom."

"How did you know it was me?" Enid asked.

"Oh, I have super powers. Mom, your name came up on my phone. How nice of you to call. What's up?"

"It's Julia," Enid said forlornly.

"Is she okay?"

"Yes. But she moved out without ever telling me she was leaving. I had to learn about it from one of the residents. I must have done something to hurt her badly for her to do that," Enid said as she began to cry. "I even talked with Hortense, the manager, and she has no idea where Julia went. She did say that Julia promised to contact her later after she was settled. Why do I annoy her so much? She must really hate me."

"Mom, stop that. You always take the blame for everything Julia does. Now, settle down. Did she have an argument with anyone?"

"Not that I know of. In fact, she had become friendly with one of the other residents. Dr. Samuel Long. I had hoped he would help her change her attitude—but he didn't."

"This doctor fellow—what do you know about him?"

"He's a history professor—grumpy and disagreeable most of the time. A funny thing—he moved, too. Nigel tried to help him, but he wouldn't even speak to him."

"Mom, do you know if Samuel had any strange… proclivities or habits?"

"My goodness, no. He has a cat that's as egotistical as he is," Enid said as she chuckled.

"When I was home the other month, Aunt Julia and I had a bit of a run-in. I have a feeling that that may be the cause of her move. Mom, let me see what I can uncover and I'll get back to you. Meanwhile, relax. Julia's probably annoying someone else by now. By the way, what about Roger?" Helena asked.

"Julia's son? Now why on earth would I contact him?" Enid questioned.

"He certainly would know where she went. Oh, oh, maybe she decided to take Roger's offer to live with him. I hope not. That could bring an end to his marriage," Helena laughed.

"Do you think Julia and Samuel could be together?"

"It's hard for me to imagine that anyone would choose to live with *that* woman. Look, let me check into this. You have nothing to worry about, Mom. You know how often that woman has moved in the past—at least a dozen, I believe. Now, join some people for dinner tonight. Relax and have fun."

"Well, I'm meeting Nigel tonight."

"What? You mean that jolly fellow who wants to come to Vegas? Mom, are you keeping something from me?" Helena asked mirthfully. "I better fly home again and check this guy out."

Enid laughed. "Not to worry—we're just friends."

"Yeah, I remember that's what I told you when I met that guy who had all those tattoos. I've got to run, Mom. We're running a slot contest today so we're really busy, but I'll call you later tonight. I promise I won't call you after ten your time. Love you. Say "hello" to Nigel for me," she said as she hung up.

CHAPTER 42

Hortense had called a meeting to discuss the makeup of the Mayors Council. Ellie May, Celeste, and Sally were seated at the table, waiting for Frank and Marty to arrive.

"Well, you know how it is with newlyweds," Hortense laughed, "It's difficult for them to get settled down to a routine. As far as MGH is concerned, there never have been so many changes being made as there has been lately. We've lost Julia and Samuel and we're still not sure why they left. I'm assuming that Frank will be moving in with Marty so that will give us three vacant apartments. However, we do have several suitable applicants on the waiting list so I don't anticipate having these too long. But, then again, one of our residents may be interested in Frank's place since it's one of the larger apartments."

"Sorry," Frank said as he and Marty entered the office. "we lost track of time since we were engrossed in reading our congratulatory notes we received at our wedding. We apologize."

"Welcome back," Hortense purred. "I hated to bother you but since the monthly Council meeting is scheduled for tomorrow I thought it prudent that we have our act together before the residents come to the meeting. I know that the Council operates on its own without any supervision from administration, but I have some suggestions for you. You could meet with a temporary appointment for Snapdragon, or you could hold an election for mayors early. Perhaps you may want to postpone the meeting until the week after the bazaar."

"Since many of us are busy with preparing for the Harvest Moon Bazaar I think we would appreciate not having to get involved in an election right now," Frank stated. "We could ask Ben to sit in—he's a always so willing to help with everything. I can still represent Orchid until the election is held. But now that I've had time to think about it, I really like the idea of just postponing the meeting. It sounds like the easiest tactic."

"Sally and Celeste," Ellie May said, "how does that sound to you?"

"That's okay with me. We're not that formal anyway," Sally replied.

"I agree," Celeste said. "Later on, I think we need to try to shake the bushes a bit. By that I mean we need to get some others involved—you know—the ones who always hang back."

"We each could take care of our own lanes. We could go door to door—you know, like in a real election," Ellie May offered. "As soon as the bazaar is over, we can get busy on stirring up interest in serving on the Council."

"I think you've solved the problem," Hortense said. "We'll post a notice in *The Square* to notify the residents," Hortense said as she stood. "Thank you so much."

"You know what I heard?" Sally asked, "Well, I heard that Julia and Samuel ran away together to California."

Hortense smiled. "I'm not too sure we should rely on rumors. I'm certain that I'll be hearing from Julia before too long. Remember, folks, I won't be able to reveal any personal information that I uncover. Of course, you understand that."

As the council members were leaving the office, they saw that Enid was waiting to see Hortense.

"Come in, Enid." When they were seated, Hortense said. "How may I help you, my dear?"

Enid wasn't certain how she should begin this conversation. She didn't want to pry in anyone's business but she was worried about her friend. "I have some concerns about Catherine. Several times lately, she has become lost and doesn't seem to remember where she lives."

"You have good reason to worry. Her family is aware that there may be a problem. Her doctors have changed some of her medication and they're hoping that a new regiment might solve her confusion. She's so insistent about participating in the Harvest Moon Bazaar that they are hoping her condition won't worsen in the next few days. Catherine's very lucky to have such a dear friend as you." Hortense said tenderly. "Her family will be spending more time here with her to assure her safety. Please keep what I have told you confidential. Above all, we don't want Catherine to hear any of this."

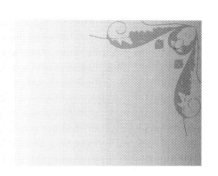

CHAPTER 43

Rosebud was stirring her coffee at a rapid pace as she finished her breakfast in the newlyweds kitchen. "But, Marty, I'm not sure I want the responsibility that goes along with being a mayor. You know, Phillip loves to travel and I really don't want anything that would interfere with going with him. I know that Sally's a poor excuse for a mayor, but I'm not sure I would be any better."

"Anyone's better than Sally. I know who would make a great mayor and that would be Abigail. Talk about a go-getter—that's Abigail," Ellie May advised.

"I think you're right, Ellie May. I don't know why I didn't think of Abigail right away," Marty said. "We've got to get someone from Marigold to nominate her.

"I'd like to see either Harry or Harvey run for mayor of Orchid. Either one of those men would make an ideal mayor," Frank surmised. "We don't have much time, the meeting is tomorrow so we need to get to work now. Rosebud, how about you paying a visit to Abigail to make sure she would agree to serve?"

"Okay. I'll do that," Rosebud agreed.

"I'll visit Ben and the Hamiltons to get their approvals. If we can get our ducks in line quickly enough we may be able to pull this off. I feel that our Mayors Council needs to become more active in policy making. And, since we won't have to worry about Samuel any longer, we may be able to make some significant changes around here," Frank reasoned. "But, let's hold off until after the bazaar. We only have three more days to prepare."

"Barry said that we'll know by tomorrow where our space will be. He's going to put up a large schematic in the lobby. I really won't need too much space for my cookies," Ellie May giggled. "I'll have little decorated boxes to put my cookies in this year with my name on—my son's idea."

"I heard that one lady from Johnson's will have all kinds of aprons—for kids and adults. I was told they're gorgeous. Ellie May, you better check her table out," Rosebud kidded.

"Abner Fulton, you know, the guy who makes jig-saw puzzles, is bringing dozens and dozens of puzzles. I'll bet he'll sell out early," Marty predicted.

"Frank, I know you've made a dollhouse. May we see it?" Rosebud pleaded.

"Okay, but close your eyes," he directed as he hurried away. "Okay, open them."

Ellie May and Rosebud were shocked. It was the most unusual dollhouse either one of them had ever seen. "It's more of a beach house than a city house" Frank explained. "See, it even has a swimming pool, a tennis court, and a sand box."

"Must people bid on the house?" Rosebud inquired.

"No, I'm going to sell chances at five dollars each. I figure I could earn more money for the Children's Hospital by selling chances. If I can sell 500 chances, I can earn $2500. There aren't many people who could afford to pay that much for a dollhouse."

"Marty, are you submitting anything this year?" Rosebud asked.

"I'm borrowing from Frank's idea. I'm taking one of my special dolls and selling chances on her for only one dollar each. I can't wait to see how it goes. Maybe Barry will let us share the same exhibit table," Marty grinned.

"Before you ask," Rosebud said. "No, I'm not submitting anything. But I promise I will visit as many exhibit tables as I can and I will spend, spend, spend. Since Phillip is representing The Children's Hospital this year, I know he'll be very busy, but I'll have lots of time to shop."

CHAPTER 44

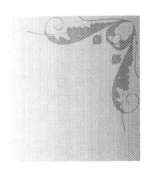

Enid was sitting on the edge of her bed looking over the booklet that Harvey had created about her teapots. While she had prepared the descriptions of the teas and the pots, Harvey was the one who designed the cover and planned the layout. The photos that Harry took were phenomenal. The colors were bright and appealing. She couldn't be more proud. Now what she had to do was to be a good saleslady and get people to sit down at her tables, drink tea, and make some purchases. She had all the teapots wrapped and stacked on a flatbed ready to be wheeled to the conference center in the morning.

She jumped when the phone rang. "Hi, Mom," a familiar voice said.

Sweetheart! I was just sitting here admiring my book. Harvey and Harry did a fantastic job. I'll see that you get a copy."

"What do you mean—a copy? I'll need at least a dozen to give out to my friends. My Mom's a famous author—I need to brag a bit."

"Oh, Helena. The boys did most of the work,"

"Hey, you own the literary property. They helped, but it's your book, Mom. Now, get ready, I need to talk to you seriously."

"My God, are you okay?" Enid whispered.

"Yes, Mom. This is about Aunt Julia."

Enid took a deep breath. "Go ahead,' she said with trepidation.

"I remembered that you mentioned Nigel offered to help the Doctor move. Now, don't say anything until I am finished, okay? It took some doing but he finally filled me in and it was just as I had suspected. You see, Mom, Julia has been dressing up as a little girl for a long time. She would put on ruffled dresses and panties and patent leather shoes. I knew for years that she was doing this—I had caught her red handed. Well, Nigel had been suspicious of Samuel for some time and, on the day of Marty's wedding, he caught them in the storage room in the garage dancing and cavorting in front of mirrors. He didn't want to report them because he didn't want to hurt you, so he sort of encouraged them to move. Mom, this should tell you something about this man. He could have been a big shot, telling everyone and embarrassing both of them, but he didn't. Mom, Nigel is your hero. There are just not many heroes like this around— you are a lucky woman."

CHAPTER 45

Barry had been working for weeks getting the conference center ready for the Harvest Moon Bazaar. While the event was a joint effort of three retirement facilities, the heaviest workload fell on MGH. A total of 58 spaces, of varying sizes, were needed—some requiring access to water or electricity, or both. This had been no easy task. Some exhibits only required a small table and a chair, others needed much more square footage. Early on, he had realized that he would need the expertise of Harvey and, as it turned out, Barry was more than willing to turn over the leadership role to Harvey who had been astute enough to bring Mary Beth in on the planning. She was the one who would be dealing with each exhibitor to inform them where their space was located, the size of the space, and the facilities they would have at their disposal. While Barry had posted the numbers for MGH residents in *The Square*, Harvey felt that a personal touch would set a friendlier tone. And, whatever Harvey needed, Barry was smart enough to make sure he got.

As Harvey and he walked the aisles of the exhibit hall at four in the morning they rechecked each space to make certain that exhibitors would be pleased. Pre-sales of entry tickets for the general public already stood at over 800. Exhibitors would be allowed to enter the conference site at seven in the morning. Since the doors would open for the general public at 10, that would give them three hours to get their spaces ready.

Barry had been getting calls and emails from all over the Commonwealth, as well as from out-of-state. People were amazed when they learned that exhibitors were donating their wares and that all money taken in was earmarked for the Children's Hospital Benefit Fund. Barry was aware that several broadcasting companies would also be arriving to interview exhibitors and organizers. He had taken extra care in getting dressed since he might be seen on TV across the nation.

When assigning spaces they had made certain that similar types of merchandise and services were not all lumped together. "I want visitors to be able to see, feel and touch the merchandise," Harvey insisted. "The key to success is customers must be motivated to buy. Every dollar coming in will help a child who needs specialized medical care. This is a very unique happening. Not only are the exhibitors extremely generous, they have put their hearts and souls into their products—something that money simply cannot buy."

"This is going to hit the national news tonight. What a wonderful way to recognize all the people who have been more than willing to work so hard to bring this event to fruition. I cannot wait until we find out just how much money we're going to be able to give to the hospital," Barry said.

As Harvey scanned the list, he boasted, "Barry, we have three people who will be selling jewelry, four artists who have a variety of paintings, large and small, pottery, baby clothes, Christmas tree decorations, wooden toys, pillows, afghans, handbags, and on and on. By the way, Carlton Swift, from United Trust Bank, will be here to act as the treasurer. When exhibitors close their tables, they will place the money they earned in a numbered bank bag. It will be Carlton's responsibility to total all funds and deposit them in the bank. In addition, we'll have two officers from our local police department—to provide the protection he needs."

"Do you know who the judges are?" Barry asked.

"All I know is that the three of them are from Craft Fairs Association. The top prize will be for the most unusual entry which I think could easily go to Enid. The winner will get $500 and will be featured on the cover of their next magazine. The other two awards will be for honorable mention. Those winners each get $250. So, I really don't want to get mixed up with any of the judges."

Just then the doors opened and exhibitors began pouring in. There were flatbeds, carts, and even baby carriages filled with merchandise. At the end of the crowd, Catherine and her son Leonard, were waiting patiently. "Mom, we'll wait until the crowd thins out."

"But, suppose someone takes my spot?" Catherine argued as she looked around nervously.

"No one will take your spot. You're number ten in the first row. You'll be okay, Mom," Leonard tried to keep her calm. "You won't have to stay here all day. People will be bidding on your quilt. When the exhibit hall closes, we'll check the box to see who put in the highest bid. And, I'll see to it that that person gets the quilt," Leonard explained patiently. "By the way, Mom, you did a great job. Your quilt is beautiful."

Ellie May passed Catherine and waved. She was anxious to get her cookies arranged attractively and was pleased that she was assigned space eight in the first row. While she had been baking for days and days, she will probably be sold out by noon. That will give her plenty of time to walk the aisles and shop. She thought she might be lucky enough to find some pretty things to use for Christmas presents.

Nigel had gotten permission to go into the exhibit hall through the rear door. He had his portable dance floor stacked on a flatbed and he was smart enough to get two of his nephews to help him lay it out. At first he had felt silly in his tails, but Enid told him that the ladies would appreciate the outfit. It didn't take long to lay out the dance floor so he treated his nephews to an early lunch—of course, he had lunch too.

Ellie was watching as Catherine's son began to arrange his mother's exhibit table. When Ellie May spied the quilt in shades of white, pink and gray, she almost fainted. There were the napkins she had been looking for. Ellie May couldn't take her eyes off the quilt that Leonard had arranged over a wooden holder. The quilt was quite eye-catching with morning glories embroidered in the white blocks, while the pink ones were plain. A one-inch gray border separated the blocks.

Now that she found the napkins, she needed to do something—but what? Picking up her cell phone, she cupped her hand around it and whispered, "Rebecca...its Ellie May...I found your napkins...hurry to the exhibit hall... aisle one, space ten...you need to see this."

When Rebecca arrived, she casually looked at the quilt. Then she turned around to speak to Ellie May. "Listen, I see and I understand. Did you know that Catherine's Parkinson's has gotten worse during the past few weeks? Yesterday, I found her sitting in the dining room at midnight, waiting for her dinner. Look at her Ellie May. She's smiling and she's very happy that I admired her quilt. Let's see how this plays out. She doesn't have to know what she's done. If no one bids on the quilt, I will. Please don't say anything to her son, let me handle that. Ellie May, I appreciate your call."

Ellie May sank down into her chair. She hadn't been aware that Catherine was having a medical problem. Ellie May was disgusted with herself. After dealing for several years with her husband fighting the same disease, how could she not have recognized the symptoms? All the time she had spent looking for the napkin thief has led her to someone who's suffering from Parkinson's. When she looked at Catherine, she noticed the blissful look on her face. If Catherine was now at some place where she felt safe, somewhere where she was not aware that something was not right, Ellie May would be content. She would not think of hurting Catherine. She walked over to table ten and told

Catherine how much she liked the quilt. As she walked back to her own table, she said, "I'm going to put a bid in for your quilt. Wish me luck," Catherine blew her a kiss.

Ellie May wiped the tears from her eyes, just as the bell rang, and the general public began entering the exhibit hall and organized chaos began.

While the crowd was large, they fanned out and soon all the exhibitors were busy showing off their wares and talking with customers. Enid was surprised that her chairs were almost immediately filled with customers eager to taste the teas she was featuring. With exhilaration that almost overwhelmed her, Enid was discussing teas and teapots to her heart's delight.

Frank's beach house was creating a great deal of interest. As the children were peeking inside the little widows, and oohing and aahing at the furniture, the adults were purchasing chances. The chances on Marty's little doll were also rapidly flying off the table.

One woman was walking along pulling a suitcase on wheels. When she stopped at Ellie May's table, she quickly purchased four dozen cookies and carefully put them inside. "Ellie May," she purred, "you're the best cookie maker in the world."

In the far corner, Nigel was teaching the rumba to his first customer of the day. He secretly hoped that he would have the stamina to keep on doing this until five o'clock, closing time.

As exhibitors sold out, they put their receipts in a money bag and carried it to a side room where Carlton was waiting. As he began counting, and more and more bags stuffed with cash and checks poured in, he came to the realization that this event could possible net more than fifty thousand dollars. He certainly was grateful that he had police protection sitting right beside him.

When personnel from the television station started arriving, excitement filled the air. The reporters didn't have any problems finding people who wanted to be on camera. It wasn't long before they had cornered Barry and Harvey who graciously participated in an interview, giving all the credit to the exhibitors.

Enid was talking with some customers when two men and a woman approached. The woman stepped forward and said, "Mrs. Murphy, I am Wilhelmina McHenry, and this gentleman is Horace Grove, and this man is Clyde O'Mara. We're the judges from the Craft Fairs Association. It is our honor to award you first place. Here's a check for $500 and, with your permission, we'll take your photograph and use it for the cover of the next issue of our magazine. We love your display of teapots and your little informative booklet is extremely creative. Congratulations!"

Enid had a difficult time finding her voice. "Oh, my, thank you…thank you very much."

Wilhelmina pinned the blue ribbon on Enid's jacket. "Do you mind holding one of your teapots in your hand while Clyde takes your photograph?"

With a smile on her face, Enid picked up her Brown Betty and posed for the camera.

The judges moved on and presented one Honorable Mention award to Frank for his doll house and the other went to Catherine for her beautiful quilt.

When the bell rang indicating that it was closing time, people scurried to make their final purchases. Rebecca and Ellie May returned to Catherine's table to be present when the highest bid would be revealed.

Leonard brought his mother back into the exhibit hall to open the bid box and announce who had submitted the highest bid. "Look, Mom, you won a ribbon."

Ellie May said excitedly, "There's an envelope, too. She also won $250!"

Catherine hung onto Leonard's arm so tightly, that he had a difficult time going through the bids. "Well, Mom, do you know Phillip Dandridge?"

Catherine pulled her brows together. "I think I do, but I'm not sure,"

Ellie May winked at Leonard. "Catherine, that's Rosebud's friend."

"Oh, yes…a good looking man," Catherine responded, with a smile.

"Mom, he bid one thousand dollars!" Leonard reported excitedly. "Mom, how about that?"

"My, that's a lot of money," Catherine said as she laughed.

Rebecca was standing in the back. She was delighted. Her dining room napkins could not have been put to better use. Leonard looked over the crowd, and to Rebecca, he mouthed, "Thank you." Rebecca waved her hand and smiled.

Enid had finished packing up her teapots when Harvey stopped by. "Harvey, would it be okay for me to leave these boxes here for a little while, I would like to go back to Nigel."

Harvey didn't ask why she wanted to see Nigel, he already knew. "Enid, I'll take the cart back to your apartment and put it by the door."

Enid quickly thanked Harvey and hurried down the aisle. When she reached Nigel's dance floor, he was just beginning to take up the boards.

"Hey, there Mr. Nuggett, you have another customer here," she said coyly.

Nigel was surprised. "And what dance would you like to learn?"

"Oh, the waltz. I want something romantic," Enid said as she openly blushed.

Nigel almost tripped over himself trying to get to his recorder. Then he spied the ribbon. "Enid, you won—you won! How wonderful."

As he approached Enid, she purred, "Just a moment. I have something for you." She reached in her pocket and pulled out a shiny badge that said *My Hero* and pinned it on his jacket. She put her arm on his shoulder and whispered, "Helena told me…no don't look away, Nigel. Look at me. You *are* my hero. Now, let's waltz."

Just then, a reporter and a cameraman were leaving the building. When the reporter spotted the elderly couple dancing, he whispered, "Get that shot—it'll be our lead-in tonight."

EPILOUGE

Let's see what Morning Glory Hill looks like three years from now when they celebrate their 5th anniversary.

- Marty and Frank have opened a doll museum called *Gretchen's Place.*
- Rosebud has moved to Maui where she and Phillip are the proud owners of a macadamia nut farm.
- Ellie May appeared on *The Martha Stewart Show* as a guest chef.
- Enid has finally turned Nigel into a tea drinker.
- William and Abigail still make beautiful music together but now as Mr. and Mrs.
- Celeste is now taking courses in librarianship.
- Gordon lost his beloved Marie and has moved back to Nassau.
- Ben had his eyebrows trimmed and is now head of the Mayors Council.
- Harvey and Harry have jointly written a book entitled *Love is Possible.*
- Samuel moved to Alaska and hasn't been heard from since. It is rumored that a polar bear put an end to

Samuel's grouchiness. It is also rumored that now the polar bear is grouchy..

- Nigel claims that Julia is giving lessons on how to get people to dislike you. You need to take the source of this statement into consideration.
- Hortense has written a book entitled *How to Run a Happy, Crazy Retirement Facility.*
- Sally, who had always wanted to be first, was the first one to pass away.
- Stretch now owns three horses and is the talk of the racetrack.
- Helena is now the CEO of Vegas' newest casino where Nigel is a frequent visitor.
- Rebecca is engaged to Stretch.
- Catherine lost her battle with Parkinson's. Remarkably, her lovely quilt found its way back to her and they left this earth together.